PANCHO TOOK THE FISH

by Rusty Jaquays

Pancho Took the Fish

Rusty Jaquays

Pancho Took the Fish/Rusty Jaquays — 1st ed.
ISBN 978-0-578-84516-6 (Softback)

This story is dedicated
to my daughter,
Lauren Ava Jaquays
"Love never dies"

PREFACE

With a strangely satisfied smile, he skipped over the bodies and onto the dock.

Just as he believed his crimes were a success and his fortune secure, his head was jerked around by flashing blue lights bouncing off the low-lying clouds.

They lit up the entire east side of the island.

In an instant, his adrenaline switched its flow away from his blood lust and began to fuel his rattling fear. Such a massive amount of law enforcement could only mean one thing.

He had just lost more than a ton of Peruvian pink-flake cocaine, worth tens of millions. This would directly connect him with the murders.

Like a silent demon, he ran across the dark parking lots, and through the back yards. Other -than the barking of a dog, and the panting of his swift shadow. He fled the scene unnoticed.

THE OLD FISHERMAN

The golden edge of a rising sun simmered on the vast ocean horizon. Rainbow colors rose up through the distant layers of clouds. What was left of the night gave way to the blue. The first light crawled across the harbor and the salty air hovering over the fishing marina was flavored with the hungry smells of coffee and bacon. A few sleepy voices carried soft through the mist.

The old, barefoot fisherman stood on the splintery wooden dock and threw his bait net. It flew from his hands, making a good circle. The quiet of the morning was awakened by the smack and a splash that launched rounds of ripples spreading outward across the slick calm water. Sebastian paused long enough to let the net sink and just before it hit the bottom his wrinkled, leather hands pulled the rope that closed the bag. He gathered it in and shook the still swimming bait fish into an old rusty bucket. With the net folded over his shoulder, he walked back to the small boat he called home. He lifted the heavy lid of the large cooler and put his catch on ice. Then he stepped into the open cabin to make his potent Cuban coffee.

It was a cramped space with an old smell but it provided shade from the blazing afternoon sun and stayed dry when it rained. Beneath the side window there was a small galley just big enough for a two-burner stove. A single shelf above the small sink held his cooking supplies and a seasoned black iron skillet hung from a well-placed nail. Up front at the helm there was a brass compass mounted on a gyroscopic base. Sitting still for years, it had grown a green patina around the edges but the smart instrument had led the old fisherman through his life at sea. Most importantly, it made sure he always found his way home. Down below, there was a stuffy bunk, just big enough for him to crawl into and sleep. If the weather was clear he could open a hatch on the bow and allow a cooling sea breeze to pass through, carrying with it the sound of the old man's snoring.

Sebastian had few possessions. But in his mind, what he owned was everything he needed. A few years back, his ancient boat motor had reached the end of its repairable life so he took it as a sign it was time to retire. The fishing marina was kind enough to give him dock space along with access to fresh water and what little electricity he needed.

He had a large family, most of them living close by. Whenever they would visit, someone always tried to convince him to come live in one of their nice houses. They had plenty of room and lots of love to offer but the old fisherman was quite content with his small and simple life. He always smiled to the concern of his loved ones. Quietly in his mind, it annoyed him to think of making any changes at this point in his life. Behind his shiny eyes lived the wisdom of his age. After a busy life that had passed by so quicky he felt that if he took everything slowly and avoided any unnecessary drama the easy pace would make his days, and nights feel longer. He was content to linger in quiet peace and savor every second of still being alive.

He usually spent the biggest part of his days watching the younger fishermen go about their work. This was not an ordinary marina, a home to sport boats or pleasure craft. Fishing from here was rarely done with a rod and reel. It was a harbor for the commercial fishing fleet where a unique group of characters harvested large amounts of seafood for the market.

Catching fish is always exciting, but pulling a paycheck out of the ocean was body breaking work. Much of it is done on land to prepare for the challenge that was waiting offshore. Behind the boats there was a labyrinth of lobster traps stacked in different stages of repair or new construction, a relentless responsibility, crucial to staying in business. A few of the bigger boats used their work area to stretch and mend long shots of gill nets, getting ready for the next big run of King Mackerel.

Once the fishermen leave safe harbor, they were committed to finishing the job despite the weather that often proved to have a multiple personality disorder. Sometimes working the deck felt like riding a surf board and operating dangerous equipment at the same time. The risk of injury or even death was an accepted part of the job. Perhaps part of the alure of commercial fishing.

The wild ocean was a fascinating world of living water. When her mood was sweet, and calm she offered a fresh understanding of freedom, her beauty overwhelming, giving the euphoria the fishermen craved. At any given time, despite the forecast, the sky could quickly turn into a black and purple whirlwind, whipping the seas into a terrible frenzy. Just a reminder that she was too vast for the imagination and the fishermen were too small for her to notice. She could swallow them quick and whole if it was her whim. Even the most seasoned fishermen lived with the kind of fear that would make their teeth chatter. Facing that fear was what grew their respect and it was that respect, coupled with a good bit of luck, that just might allow them a long life of tempting the ocean for a small piece of her bounty. Only a fierce and independent breed of people knowingly chose this way of life. It was, for most, a calling. They understood the danger but embraced the excitement and adventure that came with the job. There was a truth about some people having salt water running through their veins.

It was the adventure that Sebastian missed, but his younger days of sweat and adrenaline had left him with plenty of vivid stories to replay in his mind or perhaps tell others who might listen.

Sebastian sat on the gunwale sipping a small cup of strong

coffee, watching the sunrise. Deep in thought and reminiscence he still noticed every sound, every movement. With little baggage to clutter his mind all of his senses were able to tune into the moment. Occasionally he would shift his eyes to the crunch of the crushed shell road that ran alongside the dock. He would give his nod to the different cars and pickup trucks of fishermen steadily showing up to work. He missed nothing. Not even the gracefully gliding pelican who botched his picture-perfect landing on a nearby piling, teetering on one leg until his clumsy bulk fell head first, flapping into the water. Nobody else would have noticed the comic wink from nature but Sebastian's easy smile turned into a quiet little chuckle as though it was only meant for his eyes to see. He faced the wind and looked to the sky. Closing his eyes, he could feel what the weather would probably do.

When he finished the coffee, he opened the cooler and pulled out the fresh bait fish. Then he climbed on top and did something any passerby might have thought was rather strange. He stood holding one of the baitfish by the tail high above his head and he waved it back and forth. As he swayed, he softly sang an old Cuban love song, one he remembered from his youth. Una paloma blanca…

He wasn't crazy. This was a normal part of his routine, and he knew exactly what he was doing. He was trying to catch the attention of one particular large white bird, one that was usually hunting in the shallows across the harbor.

Pancho had a long yellow beak and stilts for legs. The great white heron stood motionless in the reeds. He used stealth, expending little energy to harpoon the food he always needed. His crystal eye locked onto the kindly human, waving his arm in the distance.

Most every morning at about this time, the easy meal was there for the taking. Wasting no time on decision, Pancho opened his long, angled wings. With an easy effort he pushed down on the air, a "whoosh-whoosh" surrounded him and with a few accelerating flaps he found the wind. He was able to glide the rest of the way across the basin. There was already a swarm of screaming seagulls begging for the pilchard in the old fisherman's hand. But when Pancho back flapped onto the cooler, they scattered to make way for the bigger, more powerful bird.

Sebastian shooed away a few of the more persistent gulls. Then with a slight bow he held out his hand.

Focused only on the fish, Pancho darted his head from side to side, naturally suspicious, but confident that it was his. In less than an instant his crooked neck unfolded and he snatched the life-giving protein. He swallowed the gift head first and for the next few minutes a fish shaped lump worked its way down his throat. As the slow-going morning merged into the day the two unusual friends quietly shared the small space on the stern of the old boat. At least, as long as the free fish kept coming.

It was rare for a wild bird like the heron to be this comfortable so close to the boats. They had a tendency to startle easily and avoided the noise and strange behavior of humans. A little more than a year before Pancho had landed on the water to rest his tired wings. Floating just beneath the surface, there was a large discarded nest of clear fishing line. When his legs became tangled, he was confused by what he couldn't see and began to panic. In the grip of his fear, he rolled several times and became hopelessly bound and doomed to drown.

Sebastian had noticed the life and death struggle on the surface of the water. From his skiff he carefully lifted the desperate, wild bird onto his lap. Holding it firmly under his arm and lightly stroking its back, he pulled a folding knife from his pocket and opened it with one hand. With smooth and gentile movements, he cut away the deadly mess.

Releasing the shivering bird, he named it Pancho.

Driven purely by instinct the bird resumed his continuing hunt for food. He kept little memory of his brush with death or of the lucky rescue by the old human, but he was marked by the loss of several feathers from one of his wings, making him recognizable among other seabirds of his kind. Whenever Sebastian caught a glimpse of Pancho soaring nearby, he would stop whatever he was doing and try to coax him closer with a bait fish.

For months, the offering went unnoticed, but the old fisherman never let himself be discouraged. He continued on with slow and steady persistence. He knew well that gaining the trust of a wild creature would come in its own time, not much different than finding trust between people.

Eventually, the beautiful bird would cautiously land on the boat, but still kept his distance. With the patient passing of a few more days Pancho would finally eat from Sebastian's hand.

THE GRINGO WHO
CALLS HIMSELF SHORTY

It was well into the morning when Sebastian heard a different sounding motor entering the harbor. He turned to see a sleek new lobster boat idle past the fish house.

He was familiar with all of the usual boats that used the marina. It wasn't often that someone new would enter. It was a rare chance for his curiosity to have something new to dwell on, so he watched to see what the fancy boat was doing in a marina for work boats.

Pancho was preening his feathers, and couldn't care less.

The stranger idled close by and then reversed into the empty dock space next to the old fisherman's boat. Pancho, agitated with the noise and smoky exhaust of the bigger vessel, angrily squawked, fussing at the rude interruption to his pleasant morning. Yet his single mindedness made him reluctant to leave the easy source of food. When the loud motor shut down, a tall young captain ducked his head and emerged from his cabin. His close proximity to Pancho was more than the skittish bird could handle. He launched into the air, dropping one of his treats into the water. Without looking back, he fled to the other side of the harbor.

One of the alert seagulls quickly dove and made the lost fish his own.

Sebastian was careful to look unimpressed, a not so friendly acknowledgment for someone who appeared to be his new neighbor at the docks. He lit his old tobacco pipe, pretending to ignore what was going on, but with a casual glance he couldn't help but notice how agile the big young man seemed to be. Docking a boat this size, especially in the breeze, was a two-man job. It was obvious that the new captain had some experience and he certainly owned a fine vessel. Considering the price of a boat like this one Sebastian wondered if the newcomer was really a fisherman at all.

During the late seventies and early eighties in the Florida Keys it wasn't uncommon to see a pretty new fishing boat that caught few fish. The country was developing a big appetite for cocaine, much of it smuggled through the hundreds of hidden waterways and uninhabited islands of South Florida. A good place for the dark business. The constant coming and going of so many boats, especially the commercial vessels and their daily activity off shore, made a perfect cover for the illegal drug providers.

Though most of these dangerous types were foreign nationals, they would sometimes lure a few of the more reckless locals to join them in the high crimes. The temptation of big chunks of fast cash was hard for some to resist.

Most of the traditional fishermen knew better than to risk their beloved freedom for the claustrophobic cage of a jail cell. To be confined and forced to stare at four walls would kill their spirit.

If something suspicious happened around the docks it was always best to either look the other way or simply leave the area. It wasn't wise to cross the killers who dealt in the drug trade. All too often the violence that came with huge amounts of dark money would spill into the world of peaceful working people. Sebastian shuddered to think of the stories he had heard and a few of the things he'd seen

The old fisherman's instincts were dependable. There was no alarm in the voice that reliably whispered in his head. The new arrival seemed to have a soft aura and an honest smile.

After the young captain hooked onto the mooring and tied off the spring lines, he turned and nodded to the old fisherman. With a friendly voice he said that his name was Shorty, a nick-name that stuck to the lanky man from back in his puberty when seemingly over-night he had grown several feet. For those who didn't know that Shorty was a peaceful man his size could be intimidating so he owned the silly name, making a joke of his size. As a first impression it showed everyone that he preferred a little humor over trouble.

Commercial fishing was a tough business and had more than its share of testy, aggressive men. Never able to back down, if need be, and somewhat reluctantly, the gentle giant might use his size and strength to defend himself. He was more of a peacemaker, well known and respected for making fools out of bullies.

This was new territory for Shorty and he didn't expect to find any welcome in these parts. He knew that the locals would be slow to trust his intentions. They were mostly father-to-son fishermen who had worked these southern waters for more generations than even they knew. In their eyes, he would be a suspicious outsider only there to compete on their traditional fishing waters.

Despite what the other fishermen might feel, Sebastian had been there long enough to have seen them all come and go. The dock space next to his had been vacant for a long time. He thought it might be interesting to start seeing the face of a new personality. He believed it would bring a little excitement to his normally uneventful part of the world.

The old fisherman decided to have a little fun with the newcomer. He continued to act aloof and disinterested, but he also pretended he didn't understand English. He thought that this might frustrate the Gringo who called himself Shorty. It was only meant to be in fun.

While the tall young captain was waiting for a response to his polite introduction, the bored old fisherman took a long pull on his pipe. He savored a few long seconds of letting the smoke out. Then he yawned, and casually looked the other way.

Shorty just shrugged his shoulders and went back to securing his boat. It bothered him that the old fisherman didn't respond to his friendly gesture. At first, he thought it was rather odd, but he reminded himself that he was the new guy and shouldn't expect much more from these people. He thought about it and realized that this was someone he would be seeing most every day. He fully intended to keep his boat in that slip for a long time to come. He decided that he couldn't leave without making one more effort to engage the old fisherman.

At least he could feel that he was starting the process of fitting in.

After his boat was tied up and secured Shorty stood on the stern and jumped over to the dock. Before beginning the short walk to his new apartment, he stood beside the old fisherman's boat. Once again, he introduced himself to the old grumpy Cuban-American. This time he saw that he was being watched by those sly old eyes. Still, there was no response. He was beginning to feel a little burn in his gut and wondered if this was someone who might turn out to be hostile. This wasn't exactly the best way to start out this new life. Shorty decided to hold his ground, continuing to bother the old guy until he got some sort of reaction, even if it was a bad one. He made himself smile his way through one last introduction. This time, he repeated his name a little louder and with more enthusiasm. He was challenging the old fisherman to go ahead and speak his mind. He watched the old man's face for the slightest change.

Sebastian sat up a little straighter. He unfolded his arms and took his pipe from his mouth. His serious eyes softened for the young Gringo. Then he scrunched his face and shook his head as he quietly hissed something in Spanish.

Shorty was somewhat relieved to see that it might only be a language problem, and not someone who was predetermined to hate him. Scratching his head, as if that would make him think better, he began to search through the few words that he knew in Spanish. There wasn't much to choose from. He did know how to count, because that involved money. He knew the names of the many Cuban foods he loved. He also had a pretty good grip on the many ways to cuss someone in the Cuban dialect.

Just in case he ever needed it.

Shorty thought he might impress the old fisherman, or at least gain a little respect by putting together a few awkward sentences in Spanish. Maybe the extra effort would spark a better response, perhaps start a conversation.

But Shorty slowly began to realize that he was being had. He knew plenty of Cuban/Americans. Sometimes they would speak Spanish among themselves but every last one of them spoke perfect English. He gave Sebastian a suspicious look, threw his arms up, and started to walk away from the foolishness.

The old fisherman quickly motioned for Shorty to stop. His seriously straight lips began to ever so slowly curve upward. It was quite a few long seconds before he finished with a big toothy grin. In English, and with only the slightest trace of an accent, he told the young captain to relax, that he had heard him the first time. Then up from his belly erupted his contagious laugh. Catching his breath in-between his hysterical "he-he-hes."

Taken completely off-guard Shorty cocked his head to one side.

Although it was next to impossible to resist Sebastian's slow growing smile Shorty strained to keep a straight face. He had always loved a good joke even if it was at his own expense. He quickly decided to turn it around, just to try the nerve of this funny old guy. He glared at the old fisherman like he was a temperamental sort of man, one who wasn't inclined to have a sense of humor. When Sebastian saw the big young captain was balling up his fists and not looking very happy, he quickly gulped down his laughter. Then he looked around for a possible escape route. After all, the young captain was no less than twice his size.

It was only a matter of seconds before Shorty moved his head from side to side, melting into his own good laughter. Much to his relief Sebastian stood up and surged across the boat eager to reach for Shorty's handshake. Cheerfully he gave his own name and said that such a tall man to have a name like "Shorty" made perfect sense to him.

Shorty was relieved to feel like he was being accepted by someone in his new life. Better yet it was a person he could have some fun with. He began walking down the dock towards home, turned, and with a savvy look, said to the old fisherman; "Adios Viejo, por la manana."

Sebastian held the bowl of his pipe, lifted his eyebrows, and nodded his approval.

PAIN IS A WONDERFUL TEACHER

Shorty had relocated from a small island town, a hundred miles to the north, where he was born and raised, and the only home he'd ever known. He was just a boy when he started to hang around the commercial fish house. After school he couldn't run fast enough to reach the dock where they weighed in the fish of many kinds, every size and every color. When they dumped the lively spiny lobster onto the big hanging scale Shorty would watch in a fascinated trance. Early on, he seemed to know that he would have a life-long connection with this interesting looking crustacean, one that the locals called "crawfish." It wasn't long before the young Shorty was doing odd jobs for the fishermen. As he prepared bait and repaired the old broken traps, he was full of questions and wouldn't hesitate to ask them. Seafaring stories from the older men always held him spellbound.

He quickly developed the skills to become a mate and be

worthy of a share. He was a natural for this kind of work. Against everyone's disapproval he quit high school, but within a few short years he had his own boat and quickly rose to be one of the top producers of crawfish at his marina.

He took pride in being a respected captain in a community built on fishing. He knew the waters of the northern Florida Keys as well as he knew his own back yard. This was his world and he assumed that it would be his until his final day. He had big plans to marry his longtime girlfriend. They spoke often about raising a family in the same small town they both had grown up in. The young couple had been hand in hand since an early age. It was the first and only relationship for either one of them. Destined to be with each other forever, or so it seemed.

The labor of each day would pass quickly for Shorty as he daydreamed about having a son or a daughter, one that would continue the tradition of ocean fishing. He was the happiest of men, feeling lucky to find his purpose so early in his life.

But the unknown was the only thing that lived just beyond the horizon.

Starry-eyed and confident in their good future together, they didn't notice the smokey haze gathering in the distance. Shorty's mom had left him a modest but decent home on the north side of the island. His girlfriend moved in and they began the fun of planning a wedding. At first it was mostly sweet words, and confident laughter. They seemed to be sailing on smooth and comfortable waters.

But after a few months of playing house, little differences and unfamiliar attitudes began to make gusts out of the air that they shared. Both were relatively immature and equally stubborn. Rather than pursuing the give and take of a successful relationship each one insisted on changing things about the other. Traits that can't be changed. Traits not meant to be changed. They ruffled each other like a wind chop, soon to fold into the swells of heavy weather. Too much of their youthful passion was being wasted on bickering, leaving little of that precious energy for building a life together.

Eventually it seemed like every day had its own fight, always waiting for the slightest reason to erupt. Harsh words and looks of disappointment lashed at their love like a wild summer squall. Before long, the bond was shattered. No different than a boat breaking up on a shallow reef. There was little left to salvage.

When they decided to go their own ways, it was very tearful and yet strangely agreeable to the both of them.

Shorty had a high capacity for physical pain. After all, he was accustomed to getting banged up by the type of work that he did. But the gut grinding of emotional pain was new to him. He was hurt and had no idea how to deal with it. On top of it all he had lost his direction. It was a small enough town where he would run into her quite often. She seemed to be way too happy and always with a different guy. Though he had no intention of resurrecting their relationship he discovered the burning feeling of jealousy and this left him confused. Shorty was just too young to realize that he was plenty young enough to start over.

Then he found himself a new friend, one that had a way of stroking his self-pity.

Shorty had never been big on drinking. He just couldn't develop a good taste for it, nor did he like the dizzy feeling of being drunk. Once in a while he might take a few hits of weed but for the most part he wasn't the type to need anything more than his own good head. "High on life" is what he would say.

He discovered that after a few shots of whiskey the annoyance of these difficult times seemed to fade. The bars were enticing and called with sweet voices to the lonely young captain. They welcomed him every night before he had to face his empty home. Once he felt the hard liquor he no longer cared and nothing could bother him. He felt no pain.

Soon enough the friendly alcohol grew claws. Drinking too much became a fast, habit. After a while, the liquid feel-good began to saturate his soul.

He went from being a fun drunk to a quiet, brooding man who would look for any excuse to be confrontational. He was always either drunk or fighting off a stagnate and debilitating hangover.

Shorty was fast becoming a shadow of the stable man he used to be. Even some of his best friends were beginning to distance themselves. It wasn't typical for Shorty the "nice guy", to be negative towards anyone. He seemed unaware of how disagreeable and belligerent he was becoming. His sense of humor became a sad attempt to fix his many offenses and that hard-won reputation was running away from him.

The big money time of year was during the lobster season and lasted for eight months. Shorty was good with his earnings and he normally saved enough to get through the four months of the off season. It was a tricky time for the lobster-men. The down time was no vacation. It was all work and no pay. The land work of refurbishing the old traps and building new ones had everything to do with the next year's production.

Without realizing it, Shorty somehow managed to blow the last of his hard-earned savings in a few of the local bars. It would be a good while before he would see any new money.

After a long night of drinking and about two hours of sleep, he woke up to pee. When he glanced at the mirror, he made a double take. Startled by his red, swollen eyes peering out from his bushy face he laughed and called himself an "ugly bastard." His insides began to boil with the sickening realization that he really was broke, something he never had to deal with before. The new reality made him puke.

He tried to lie back down and make himself pass out, thinking it might all go away. His drunk was turning into a skull-crushing hangover. With his head reeling he rolled out of bed and landed on the floor. Completely aggravated with his own aggravation, he stepped into his white rubber fishing boots and staggered his way to the boat.

During the off season there were a few other types of marketable fish to be caught. They didn't pay nearly as much as crawfish, but the fisherman who ran out of money can make a small paycheck, enough to pay the bills and get by. A few king mackerel were being caught offshore just beyond the reef. Normally, the big net boats at the marina were the ones who handled this type of fishing. Shorty's boat wasn't set up to do this kind of work. He also believed that this was a wasteful way to harvest seafood. The smaller fish that escape the net are too damaged to survive, depleting the resource.

There was another method to use for a smaller and higher quality catch. It was usually done by slowly trolling four lines at different depths behind the boat, six with outriggers. Each line had a long steel wire leader attached to a shiny lure and tipped with a strip of fresh bait. When the fish are found, the boat goes into a circle and the fishermen will work all of the lines. It was like a dance, pulling one fish after the other, fresh from the seawater and onto the ice.

The wire can be as sharp as any knife and there is a certain way to snatch it without injury. This leaves little to no room for error. It's crucial that the fishermen have a clear head and quick reactions to catch the toothy fish.

Shorty didn't check the weather nor did he bother to call one of his mates to join him. He was in a wild, bullheaded mood as he pounded his boat into the growing waves. He decided to fix his hangover by taking a long swig on a partial bottle of whiskey. Even with his head hanging the wrong way he found the fish. He did well for a few hours and caught more than five hundred pounds. He took a look at the sky and noticed the worsening weather so he made the decision to catch just one more before heading in.

As he was pulling in a twenty-pounder the wire suddenly went slack. The fish had turned and was now swimming towards the boat. Shorty knew that something big in the water had zeroed in on his fish. He was angry with the thought of losing it. Instead of dropping the line and allowing a small part of his catch to feed the ocean. He quickly pulled through the loose line until he felt the fish. Just as he took a wrap on the wire to put it on board. The bull shark hit the fish at a tremendous speed.

Instinctively, Shorty braced his knees against the inside of the stern, so not to be yanked overboard. He desperately tried to free his hand from the tightening coils. There was no stopping the power and momentum of the shark. His glove was pulled off along with most of his little finger.

When he held up his hand to see the damage, the sight of his torn flesh and jagged bone immediately made him light headed and nauseous. At first there was little feeling in the frightening womb. By the time he applied a tourniquet and packed his hand in a towel full of ice, searing pain punched through the numbness in scalding waves.

He pointed the boat toward safe harbor and laid the throttle down. With one hand he struggled to hold the wheel straight in a sloppy ocean. Beginning to fade into shock, he rubbed ice on his eyes and his wrists to try and stay conscious.

He just barely made it back to the marina and the waiting ambulance.

Shorty had caught thousands of king mackerel over the years with hardly a scratch. If he was sober and had his head screwed on right, he would have reacted differently and dropped the wire the very second it went slack.

Sometimes young men have to learn life's lessons the hard way. Losing love is never easy and always painful. Instead of bucking up and moving on, Shorty believed he could drink his problems away. Pain is a wonderful teacher. His hand swelled to the elbow and his arm ached to the shoulder. The doctor told him to give it three months to heal. It was a smoldering wound with occasional sharp jags that shook his whole body, a permanent mark that would remind him of his arrogance and poor judgment every day, for the rest of his days.

SHORTY HAD NEVER
SEEN A MOUNTAIN

Sober, and with a clear head, Shorty realized how close he came to an early end. He admitted to himself that he was lucky to only lose a finger and not his life

One by one, he began to remember the dumb ass things he said and did during his binge. This made him cringe with shame and a few times he slapped himself on the side of the head. Once, he forgot to use his good hand, and the self-inflicted pain sent him to the moon.

He had a few good friends with whom to make amends and he wondered if his once sturdy reputation was even repairable. The reality that hit him the hardest was how badly he had neglected his business. He was at least three weeks behind in preparing for the oncoming lobster season. Shorty was sure to be last in the race to put his traps in the best spots. This would set him up for failure for the entire season, always one step behind the others, bringing in little more than what it takes to cover paying his mates and expenses. He had never put himself in such a hopeless position. Although he wasn't the type to quit any kind of a struggle, he couldn't seem to figure out a way to turn his precarious situation around. For the first time, he was afraid of losing his beloved business.

With opening-day coming on fast the timing of his injury couldn't have been worse. Although he had two mates, he was still a working captain. He couldn't see how it would come together without the use of both of his hands.

This was an exciting time for the people who harvest crawfish. There was the scent of a long-awaited paycheck in the air. As the big day approached, they went from a hot, lazy walk into a dead run.

As hard as Shorty tried to take control and push the progress of his work he only got in the way and slowed things down. There was little that could be done one-handed. The womb wanted to heal but everything he came close enough to bump into seemed to be aiming for his bloody bandage.

With the busy work swirling all around him, Shorty was completely flustered. All that he could do was sit back and watch. He felt like he was forced to be still in the middle of a race and it was making him crazy. He decided to ban himself from his boat and the unfinished traps, at least for a few days. It would be best for his business and he could only hope that his disillusioned mates would tough it out and keep working. They were both independent professionals who could easily leave him for another boat with more potential.

He needed some time in a quiet space to calm the worries that were ping-ponging in his head, so he could think, perhaps chart a better course.

He committed himself to spend some time at home. It wasn't long before his house felt like it was shrinking, closing in around him until he was finally squeezed out of the back door and onto his patio. The outside air was hot and humid but it felt good to be out in the open. He moved a chair to the shade and tried to find a comfortable way to cradle his aching arm. Leaning back, he closed his eyes and took a long, deep breath.

After a few hours of deep reflection, he realized that lying around, wallowing in guilt, and kicking his own ass wasn't going to fix a badly broken future. He had to come up with some sort of a new plan, something different, something drastically different.

Under the loud, ugly noise in his head, he thought he heard a soft comforting voice, one that almost sounded like his mom, but he couldn't hear the words clearly enough to know what they said.

He shook his head thinking it was weird and probably just the misfire of some of his booze-damaged brain receptors. But for a few mysterious seconds he felt calm and rather good. It unclogged his mind and took him back to another life when he was still a kid.

She was too young when she passed, so battered and frayed

from the two-job life of a single mom. Along with few bad bouts with the wrong men, the constant stress of survival made damn sure she neglected her own health. But never for a second did she neglect mothering her son. Against the odds she managed to raise Shorty to be a strong man with good intentions.

It was a hard nineteenth birthday when he buried her, absorbing that he was alone with no other family that he knew of.

Although mother and son had faced more than a few difficult times she had this way of thinking forward that always seemed to power them through, wasting little time on what was wrong and always looking for what was possible. Sometimes she would blink away the tears and muster a courageous smile, then remind her son of the old adage that "whatever doesn't kill us will surely make us stronger."

As he surfed the memories of his youth, he quickly ran out of exciting events to dwell on. He felt a little shame when he realized that his life so far wasn't all that interesting. Everything revolved around the small island town where everyone knew everyone else with only the occasional carload of tourists and their out of state plates stopping for gas or lunch.

Here he sat, well into his twenties and he had never been north of Miami. He felt a powerful pang of urgency, keenly aware that the big wide world was just passing him by. So many people and so many places only existed in his imagination. The TV and the colorful pages of magazines were his only source of knowledge beyond his simple little life.

Shorty had never seen a mountain. But he often dreamed of such magnificent things.

He did have a few memories of making trips south to Key West. It was only when his mom could take a rare day off and couple it with a weekend. Those were the highlights of his childhood.

Key West was the most delightful kind of a visual overload, filled with worldly people who celebrated their own individuality. He had crystal clear visions of their happiest times together in this colorful, musical, and very delicious island city.

Then, just like a burst of sunlight when it finally breaks through the longest gray sky, Shorty had a revelation. Since he had hit his own personal "rock bottom" wouldn't it be best to just cash everything out and begin again?

Wouldn't it be cool to make a new life in a place like Key West?

It gave his heart a pretty good jab to think of leaving his home. This was the first time he had thought about living somewhere else but nothing about his current life had any promise left, not enough to make him need to stay.

Something felt so right about the thought of starting over, setting off an explosion of exciting possibilities. He jumped out of his lawn chair, leaving the indentation of his ass on the cushion. While he paced the small patch of Bermuda grass that he called his back yard his mind went to work on an exciting new plan. Everything about such an enlightened idea made sense.

Regardless of where he went, he would always take his skills as a fisherman. The waters of the southern keys were vast and exploring the new ocean bottom would make his work feel more like an adventure.

All his life he had heard about the endless fishing possibilities around Key West and beyond. He remembered hearing stories about the hordes of spiny lobster migrating through the lower Keys from the Gulf to the Atlantic reef. He'd always marveled at the reports of huge catches, common to the Southern lobstermen.

A few weeks earlier, his first mate had offered to buy his business. At the time it made him angry to think about quitting but the mate sensed his captain's weakness and he was really offering a way out. Shorty's boat was medium size, older, but sound and he had recently rebuilt the motor. It was slow, like most lobster boats but still ran strong and would serve any experienced fisherman well.

He owned a thousand traps, half of which were seasoned from the years before. The toughest part of the job was to re-pair the damage that the ocean will put on the gear. His mates had done most of this particular work. So, he thought it would be fair to throw them in with the sale of the boat, giving them a chance to make a go of it.

He would keep the other half of his traps, the new ones most of which he had managed to build before he became lost on his drunken journey. They still needed a little more work so he would keep them in reserve for his new endeavor.

The transaction with his mate happened quickly and without

a hitch. It was a win/win for both men.

Shorty spoke to a friend who was a real estate agent on the island. He was clueless about most business types of matters. Too much arithmetic for his liking. As luck would have it, he managed to hit the market when sellers could name their price. In less than a month he closed on the sale of his property for a lot more than he expected.

It seemed too real when he said goodbye to his boat and the home where he was raised. He felt a wave of emptiness and for that moment he was unsure of himself.

His confidence quickly returned when he realized he was sitting on the biggest pile of money that he had ever seen. Sober, and finely making good use of his smarts, he talked to a banker and secured it to finance his courageous new plan for life.

How quickly his rotten luck reversed itself as soon as he committed to the big change. Everything began falling into place as if it was all meant to be. He had good reason to find his long-lost smile. It felt so good to feel good again. Maybe this was some sort of divine destiny that was just waiting for him to discover.

Like any young fisherman, Shorty had the boat of his dreams already picked out. It normally takes years of paying dues to work up to a Dream Boat, something many fishermen never achieve. He almost felt guilty for considering such a prize at his young age.

He took a road trip south in his old beat up "fish truck" to

Stock Island, just north of Key West. There, he paid a visit to one of the more renowned boat building companies and within an hour he walked out with a brand new 43-foot fiberglass boat, powered by a V12 turbo diesel engine, leaving behind a very happy salesman.

It was the biggest motor that could be squeezed into a boat of this size, lightweight but strong, built for working the sometimes shallow, sometimes deep waters throughout the Caribbean. She had beautiful lines with the capacity to carry more than a hundred traps and still be swift.

Best of all, the cabin, and bunk area were closed in and dry with sliding windows to give him a clear look around as he drove the boat.

It contained all of the comforts of home. So, if need be, it could always serve as a good back-up place to live. Although the door was cut a little low for a tall man, Shorty would just have to remember to duck, something he sometimes had a problem with. He jokingly admitted to being hard headed in more ways than one.

Shorty was too practical to want a fast boat for the sake of being fast. Crawfish are usually sold as a live product and most of the locals worked what they called "banker's hours", leaving in the morning and returning to weigh in their catch before the fish house closed at dinner time. Their slow but heavy-duty boats would compel them to work the waters closer to their home port. He knew it would be the same for the southern fishermen. It was a crucial part of his plan to extend his range further west than the others. The extra speed would make it possible to avoid infringing on the crowded areas already claimed.

He had to be careful to not offend the locals or they would make it impossible for him to succeed. He also reasoned that the more distant waters would have less fishing pressure and promise to be rich with lobster.

He was really feeling his luck when he found a nearby commercial marina that catered to lobster boats. There was only one available dock space left so he secured it, the one he didn't yet know would be next to Sebastian's boat.

He also found an apartment that was close enough to walk to his job. Now that the boat was everything that he owned, he wanted to be able to keep a close eye on it.

In a quiet moment while driving back on the bridges of A1A Shorty was able to savor the view of his shimmering, blue-green waters from above. He wondered what kind of fantastic, and probably, terrible experiences, were waiting out there for him.

Flushed with excitement. He couldn't wait to find out.

THE HOMELESS CREW

Lighter in his step than usual Shorty had goosebumps as he started the first walk to his new work place. A burst of clean energy made him feel like running but he purposely slowed himself down to notice every little thing along the path, one that he would come to use most every day. The tropical vegetation seemed to be much lusher and more colorful than it was back home. There was also more traffic and a lot more people than he was used to. But he was looking at his new life and it was no longer just a blurry, insecure vision conjured up in his daydreams.

Although his hand was still bandaged and a little stiff, enough time had passed for the healing to take hold. It was time to put it to the test by getting back to work.

It was less than a quarter of a mile from the door of his apartment to the gate of the marina. He passed a dog track, busy and well-lit during the early evenings, its parking lot empty and void of activity during the days and late nights. He saw a small store with a sandwich shop. It looked like a good place to grab a coffee and possibly meet some of the local fishermen. He was too anxious to get his boat to stop and wait in any lines.

The marina was separated by a high chain link fence topped with coiled razor wire. It looked secure but they left the gate open, night and day. The lock and chain were rusted beyond use. Apparently, locking it up became more trouble than it was worth. There was always the occasional boat coming in late or one that would want to leave early.

There was a vacant lot across from the entrance of the marina. A group of people, mingling together around a pile of stacked telephone poles, were passing a quart of beer in a brown paper bag and sharing the same cigarette.

He knew right away that they were homeless.

The lower keys had a large and diverse population of street people. Perhaps the attraction of year-round, warm weather made it more survivable than in the cold northern cities. Key West was the southernmost point and the actual end of the road. There was nowhere else to go. Over the years there was an accumulation of lost people well beyond what the local government and charitable services could handle.

Shorty felt like many of these people had brought on their own problems. As a hardworking man, he couldn't understand how anyone could be satisfied with living in the dirt, always under the stress of bare-bones survival. How could anyone's laziness overpower the natural need to be productive? There were plenty of jobs in the island city but few would hold one long enough to get over the hump and reach for a better life.

Most of them lived off of lucrative panhandling in the busy vacation town. A few might elevate themselves above common beggar by devising low talent acts, playing a pawn shop instrument or creating a set of drums out of overturned buckets and discarded pots and pans. They would set up along the sidewalks on Duvall Street and coax coins and dollars from sympathetic tourists. In a strange way they contributed to crazy splash of color that painted the picture of Key West.

Feeling like their island paradise had been invaded and over run by the outcasts of elsewhere, some of the locals were resigned to calling their home town "Key Waste" or "Key Weird" Quite a few felt like they were forced to sell their homes and leave to find a place with more normalcy. It wasn't unusual to see a sign in someone's yard that said "another conch leaving Key West".

Shorty understood that many of the homeless had serious drug and alcohol problems. Given his recent fling with a jug of whiskey he could understand how easily someone running low on purpose could be seduced by a fake feel-good. Especially during a prickly period when everything seems to be turning to shit.

Looking back, he had to thank his hard luck for snapping him back to reality. Shaking his head, he realized he might have slipped into the same hole as some of these people. He wished he knew a way to convince others that just being alive is a gift not to be wasted on being wasted.

Shorty was thoughtful and had a good measure of empathy for those who deserved it. What bothered him the most was knowing that children were sometimes cast into this shadowy and dangerous existence. He once heard a story of a shrimp boat captain who hung out at the bus station waiting for young runaways who looked lost. He would entice them with a few bucks and a sweet-sounding job on his boat. Once far enough out to sea, they would be confined only to realize the horrifying nightmare of being forced into sexual favors for the dank, dirty crew.

After weeks at sea, and time to return to port, with no remorse, these most evil of men would dispose of the badly damaged young people like garbage into the swallowing sea. Their final experience with life was the worst kind of torture.

This went unnoticed for years before anyone caught on to this blatant consumption of children. There were other stories almost as brutal. It seemed that there was no age limit for the hungry teeth of cruelty.

Shorty also knew of the forgotten ones with physical and mental challenges. From time to time these helpless innocents would slip through the cracks of mainstream society. How lost they must feel, surrounded by this confusing and unforgiving world without the ability to avoid the dangers. They became easy prey for the sharks and wolves that hunt the world of people without a home.

Shorty had an interest in everyone regardless of who they appeared to be. He was the type who gave equal consideration to all he met. Only then would he decide who to avoid or who might be worth knowing. Judging by the ground covered with cigarette butts and beer cans, it looked like a regular gathering place for the non-working people on Stock Island.

He would be passing by them, and probably others, most every day. He decided to acknowledge these castaways, to carve a few minutes from his rush to work and meet a few of the local residents without addresses. He swayed his course to the other side of the road to be friendly, maybe leave them with one of his corny jokes and gift a smile to their miserable day.

As he got closer, an older woman, who reeked of stale beer, got up and stumbled over to the fence. Her crusty looking partner lost his balance when he tried to stand and join her. He had to hold up his pants and stagger at the same time. She dropped her shorts and squatted down to pee, oblivious to the cars passing by and the people around her.

Her man put his hand on her head to keep his balance. Then he let his pants fall and joined her. When he tilted his head back to take another long gulp of warm beer he fell backwards into the fence, adding more wetness to his urine-soaked clothing. When the couple noticed Shorty approaching the corner they beamed exaggerated smiles, showing green tinted teeth. Both had gray skin in contrast to their eyes that had the yellowish color of liver damage.

Shorty stopped short in the middle of the road and strongly reconsidered acknowledging these people. There was something so silly about their behavior that kept him curious. Maybe he would be the one who would wind up with a good laugh for the day. He would be careful not to get close enough to breathe the same air. It was hard to understand the slurring, slobbering words they said, so he took charge of the conversation and gave the gross couple nick-names. If he ever saw these ridiculous people again. He would call them, "Frick and Frack."

As soon as he said the words they broke into a loud, boisterous bout of laughter, peppered with gags and snorts.

A dark-haired lady, possibly in her thirties, and perhaps a pretty girl at one time in her life, sat on one of the poles and looked down with her head in her hands. Shorty saw the long track marks on the insides of her arms. In between her spider web tattoos there was an infected crater from an overused injection spot.

The junkie looked up, sly and unimpressed.

She sat up straight when she saw the clean, nice-looking captain. She rubbed her legs and with a raspy attempt at a sexy voice she said that they called her "Sunshine." She immediately put the make in her eyes and tried on an inviting smile, making sure the potential customer knew she would be happy to do anything for a few dollars.

Shorty gave her no reason to further approach him but was careful not to sound like he was talking down to any of them.

There were a few others who were curious, and quiet. Shorty got the vibe that there might be a throat-cutter among them. Probably someone recently released through the revolving door of an over-crowded prison system, not rehabilitated or reformed to be safe for the general population. A nocturnal predator who waited for night to lurk in the shadows with ill intent.

Sitting alone on the other end of the poles was a smaller, younger looking person.

Shorty was in a hurry to get to his boat and start his day. Believing he had spent enough time on these people, he couldn't leave without walking over and having a look at this one. He felt like he needed to approach the boy like he was a small wild animal, one that might let you get near but bolt when you take that one step too close.

Underneath a mess of bushy, almost white hair naturally matting into dreads, there was a small delicate face, blistered red from the merciless sun. One of his worried looking eyes was off center and seemed to float. The fear coming from this child really affected Shorty. He felt his own heart beat as he absorbed the damage.

He took a step back, stooped to his knees and with his most gentle voice asked the boy his name. Sunshine said he was wasting his time; "the kid probably wouldn't talk. They just called him Dit-Dit. He stutters so bad he never makes any sense." She chirped a cruel sounding laugh.

Shorty snapped a harsh look in her direction, scolding her

with his eyes. She looked back at the ground, turned and made conversation with a few of the others, pretending to ignore someone who would dare to challenge her crude behavior.

Shorty noticed that she did give a sympathetic glance towards the boy. Perhaps, there was still some heart buried under her crust. He wanted to believe there was hope for everyone.

He saw that he was only making the boy more nervous by trying to be friendly. Perhaps this kid wasn't used to having someone pay him this much attention. Shorty opened his lunch cooler and pulled out a fat sandwich. He held it out with an enticing look.

He said, "Go ahead, it's yours." The boy flinched and stiffened.

He shifted his leery eyes from the food to the generous man. Shorty didn't know or care if the others were watching. He remained totally focused on his worthy mission.

For a few lingering, quiet moments, he was persistent with the offering. Then he shrugged his shoulders and acted like he had given up and was going to put it back in the lunch cooler. He noticed the kid's eyes open a little wider, still not sure if he should take what he really wanted. It seemed like he was more stuck than afraid, as though making choices was a difficult thing to do.

This kid looked normal, perhaps a little hungry and frazzled but Shorty began to have an unpleasant awareness that he must have some sort of disability, maybe autism.

Shorty made a couple of funny faces and it seemed to work.

He thought he detected just a smidgen of a smile. He tossed the sandwich, forcing the boy's reflex to catch it.

The overwhelmed kid jumped up and walked away from the rest of the group. He stood while he ate the fresh food, a rare treat, far better than the dumpster meals he was used to. Several times he cast a suspicious look over his shoulder, afraid someone might take it from him.

Indeed, the rest of the homeless crew were watching with greedy eyes, like the kid was supposed to be the last in line for any handouts. Shorty had enough street sense to stick around until the hungry child finished eating.

The drunk woman made a few clumsy attempts to get up and pee again and went directly into her business-as-usual mode. She turned around and held out her filthy hand boldly asking Shorty for some spare change. He knew it was coming so he reached into his pocket for a few coins and loose dollar bills. He counted out an equal amount, for each of them. They all praised his generosity. He realized they would just spend it towards the slow suicide of drugs and alcohol. But he was the one who chose to stop and make this curious visit. He couldn't leave them empty handed.

While they were distracted, he carefully approached the thin, fragile boy and asked if he was alright, if he needed any help. When he was sure that the others weren't looking, he pressed a ten-dollar bill into the small hand.

The kid gripped the money tight and fast stepped down the

road towards the next intersection, stopping to turn around and take one more glance at the nice fisherman. For a few seconds those severe looking eyes began to melt into the softer look of hope. Shorty began to burn with the urgency to do something more to help. Before he could think of anything, the poor kid quickly turned the corner and vanished into his uncertain existence.

The experience left Shorty deeply troubled. He stood by the road flexed and still, feeling the shame of helplessness. How could he fail to try and rescue this child with special needs? He could only hope that this kid would survive to be seen again. He promised himself that he wouldn't blow the next chance to help the helpless.

Shorty decided that one visit to the corner was all he needed. After this he would only offer a friendly wave to the homeless crew. He didn't want to be seen as a regular contributor to their survival.

He thought about the kid. The other people on the corner had chosen their situation but something really bad must have happened to this one. He would keep his eyes open for that thatch of sun-bleached hair.

THE OUTSIDER

When Shorty entered the gate to the marina and walked to his boat, he realized how lucky he was to have a slip so close to the fish house. He could carry most of his supplies without having to start up and use the boat every time he needed something. It gave him a lift to see Sebastian and Pancho relaxing into their morning. He slowed his pace and passed by carefully so he wouldn't scare away the big, beautiful bird.

Pancho was alert, keeping one eye on the giant human. His neck stretched up and he opened his wings to make himself appear bigger, a natural show of bluster when wild creatures feel fear. He looked proud of the image he was making, his feathery crest and tail fluttering in the sea breeze.

Sebastian gave a hardy greeting in Spanish to the young captain. He had a fresh pot of strong coffee and insisted on a few minutes with the newcomer before he got lost in his work. It made Shorty feel like he was welcome, but every time he tried to step onto the old fisherman's boat, Pancho would flex his wings and threaten to take off. So, he opted to stand on the dock and discuss a little fishing with his new friend. He was anxious to know more about the new waters.

After a few informative but fun minutes with Sebastian Shorty jumped on his own boat to check the engine. The abrupt noise of Shorty's big feet hitting the deck launched Pancho back into the air. He fled, soaring just above the surface of the water to a quiet, distant part of the harbor. Shorty felt obliged to apologize for scaring off Sebastian's pet bird but the old fisherman shrugged his shoulders and said that Poncho was lazy and getting too fat anyway, not to worry. He would be back the next morning looking for more free fish.

A flatbed truck pulled into the work area behind Shorty's boat. His mates from back home had finished building the five hundred new traps he held in reserve. He was happy to see his home boys and share a few laughs as they labored through the unloading of the prime gear. They told him he would be welcomed back, if things didn't work out in Key West. He thanked them for the help. He went for his wallet and made sure the effort was well worth their while.

Although his hand still wouldn't close all the way he began to load his gear onto the boat. It was awkward, and slow going. The slatted, wooden traps were more than a hundred and fifty pounds of dry weight. Each one needed to be baited with suspended flags, made with short lengths of wire and pieces of raw bull hide. The bait was greasy and tough to cut but it lasted long enough in the salt water to attract the scavenger lobster into the funnels. The more rancid it was, the better it worked. Cutting up bait with a shiny new edge on a long, rusted butcher knife was the first job of every day. Focused on the slippery chore, there was no getting used to the raunchy stink. It made the rest of the work feel delightful.

Shorty double coiled the ropes and tied on three round buoys. They were freshly painted with his specific colors; red, yellow, and orange. His lobster permit number was branded into each one. They were easy to see against the surface of the deep blue of the ocean and the light blue of sky. They would also distinguish his traps from the other fisherman's individual color combinations.

Lobster boats usually have a crew of two to four people. The captain is "the hunter." Whether he ran the boat for a silent owner or personally owned his outfit, the responsibility of safely making money was his to bear. Staying in business required skills that only come with hard experience. Finding the heaviest populations of crawfish was tricky and ever-changing. There were many factors to consider before committing the time and labor of moving hundreds of traps around a big piece of the ocean.

The weather and phase of the moon, controlled the behavior of all sea creatures. For lobster, it was also important to understand the ocean bottom. In certain conditions the lobster could be found on the jagged reefs or the hard feather bottom which would be tough on the condition of the traps. That could change when the dark nights around the new moon brought them out of hiding and allowed them to crawl over the soft sandy grass beds. These mysterious decisions are made by nature and anticipated by only the captains who are most in tune.

Once the traps are set in lines of ten, and as many as two hundred, the ones that come up blank are loaded onto the boat and reset on what they hope are more productive areas. Always trying to out-maneuver the other fishermen like a gigantic game of chess.

The mates stand at the winch, alongside of the boat and work the traps, one at a time. They have to work fast to pull the spiky, spiny creatures back through the funnels and into the sorting crates behind them, careful not to damage the product. It's a skill that comes with repetition and time. An experienced mate can empty a loaded trap in seconds while another one replaces the bait and scrubs away the mud and sea debris that is always growing, trying to consume the wooden traps.

A few times in the day they would have to slow down enough to repair one that was broken from a powerful grouper or a huge lime green moray eel that would easily break the stout traps to get to the captive lobster inside. A desirable meal for more than just people.

Sometimes the fisherman will pull a trap with a fish still inside, too fat from eating all of the crawfish to squeeze back out. Although it made for a few more minutes of work it was a good dinner for the crew. One time Shorty had two big mutton snappers come up in the same trap. He marveled at the beautiful red fish that still had spiny lobster whips protruding from their mouths. As big as they were, he wondered how they squeezed through a much smaller funnel. The overwhelming need to feed must have motivated the snapper to force their way in.

Everyone on the crew works together as one to pull as many traps in the course of a day as humanly possible. They reset them, cleaned with fresh bait, ready to fish. It wasn't uncommon for a seasoned crew to pull over three hundred traps in a day. It's fast, hard work even when the water is calm but quite a challenge when the boat is dancing on a rough ocean. At the end of the day the captain and the mates are exhausted, sometimes bleeding through their cloth gloves. Handling the lobster with sharp spines, and then scraping the razor oysters that grow between the slats and the funnels leaves them with swollen hands, cuts on their arms, and the occasional poke from the poisonous fins of a scorpion fish.

A few years back Shorty had a deep cut on his forearm. He was too engulfed with his work to stop and tend to it. He didn't notice the long clear blue tentacles of a Portuguese man of war wrapped around the trap rope. When it passed through the snatch block it slapped a long venomous piece into the raw cut, sending a hot electric burn down through his arm.

Sebastian gave him an old-fashion remedy for encounters with the poisonous species that hide among the beauty and vivid colors of the reef. If he didn't carry a bottle of ammonia on the boat Sebastian told him to pee on the wound. It would have the same effect of neutralizing the excruciating pain.

Both the captain and the crew are paid by incentive either taking a share or percentage. Money is the motivator and it makes for a good pain killer

Shorty's plan was to start working alone. He'd be driving the boat and pulling the traps. His head was clear and he was under no illusions about what he was about to get into.

He built an additional steering station into the winch box on the port side of the deck just behind the cabin where he would be able to see his gear without running over the ropes and floats. It was a real pain to have to go overboard and use a hack saw, to cut the hard plastic wad of melted trap rope from the shaft and propeller. During rougher weather he would have to create a harness of some sort to ensure that he stayed with the boat. He knew what it was like to be slammed from behind by a rogue wave. Once a person is thrown from his boat, he was no longer at the top of the food chain and wouldn't last long in a hungry ocean. It was everyone's unspoken fear.

It was well into the season and all of the good mates would already be working. He didn't want to risk any problems with this new group of fishermen by trying to lure someone from another crew. There were always a few strays looking for work around the docks but if they weren't already working, they might not be the best ones to hire. They probably wouldn't have the experience or reliability needed to stand up to this kind of a job. They were called "burnt spoons" because they worked on a day-to-day basis for their drugs.

It would be slow going and a little on the dangerous side, but for now, he was resigned to make his best effort and go it alone. He would have to work fewer traps and wait until the next season to hire a proper crew

It took a few hours to bait and stack eighty traps on the rear deck. He still had enough daylight to set them well beyond the areas crowded with the buoys of other fishermen. If he could avoid encroaching on the territory claimed by the locals the extra effort might earn him a few allies at the marina. If he started out showing respect it would eventually earn him respect.

As he idled out of his slip and passed some of the boats still moored in the marina several of the older men acknowledged him with a smile and a wave. A few others gave him the nod of approval. Whether they looked his way or not, everyone was well aware of a new player at the marina. He was tired and his hand was beginning to throb but he was quick and happy to return the greetings. He hoped that these were the beginning signs of acceptance.

As he approached the narrow mouth of the protected harbor, he could finally see the ocean beyond. For Shorty and many others, it was an exhilarating few moments when leaving the calm sheltered basin and joining the swells that rolled into the whitecaps of the open sea. When the boat began to serge there was a feeling of pleasure that was tempered with just enough fear to make them crave the challenge ahead.

Off to his right, at the far end of the lobster docks, he noticed a stout man jump from one of the boats. His fists were clenched tight and he had an angry stride. He hopped onto the rocks of the jetty and reached the sea wall just as Shorty passed.

With only a few feet between them Shorty recognized Falon, a man he had been warned about, who glared through his bristling beard and long fiery red hair. His tattoo smothered arms were crossed and flexed. He had a powerful build like the men who had spent some time in prison where they have nothing to do but lift weights all day, every day for years.

When Shorty made eye contact his friendly gesture was met with a promise of violence. Without words the look said it all, a deliberate challenge from a dangerous-looking man. It raised the hair on the back of Shorty's neck. A bit rattled, he gathered back his confidence and pressed ahead into the ocean.

Throughout the day, his positive thoughts were invaded by the quiet danger of that encounter. It was a strong reminder that he was the Outsider and, to some, he might always be.

WHEN THE CRAWFISH CRAWL

Shorty got off to a hard start.

His injury was still tender and he felt like a man would after doing the work of several men. He was more than exhausted and worried about how long he could keep it up. It took him six days to set four hundred traps. He steamed a good distance to the south west of the Marquesas islands to a remote area they called "no man's land." For now, it was wide open and only a few other fishermen had their traps here. It left him plenty of space to soak his gear.

On the seventh day, he began pulling mostly blank traps, and barely caught enough to pay for fuel. He wasn't surprised, considering his virgin efforts in this territory.

It was time to go into his hunting mode.

Over the next month he stubbornly picked up and moved his gear to different depths, and types of bottoms. It was the toughest work that he ever accomplished, nonstop, no days off, with little to show for his efforts.

Difficult periods eventually pass when the weather patterns changed, and so did Shorty's luck. As he looked down into the clear blue water his traps began coming up filled to the funnel with lobster.

Triggered by the first cold front in the late fall most of the crawfish in the Gulf of Mexico begin their migration South. When they reach the keys, they funnel together into lines, sometimes hordes, that cover the bottom. They crawl through the narrow channels between the islands congested with a gauntlet of traps. The uncaught lobster found their way to the drop-off beyond the reef where they spawn. When the crawfish crawl, the traps fill up with money. It's the prime part of the season but doesn't last long. The push between fishermen for dominance over the best bottom is now a battle.

It's a big ocean and difficult to see what other boats are doing in the distance. With only two Florida Marine Patrol boats for a hundred square miles, it was nothing short of being lawless. For a few, it was anything goes when no one was looking. Stealing lobster from each other was not uncommon.

Most of the lobstermen were too busy with their own gear to be tempted with the traps of others. They stayed on top of their own work before someone else did. But little rivalries and feuds erupted when the temptation to be greedy took over, usually among the younger, more aggressive fishermen. It became a game of getting even and often ended with a fight back on the land. A fairly common distraction around the docks.

There was a popular phrase spoken with a friendly warning: "If you snooze you lose." In other words, stay on top of your gear or somebody else will.

The few officers who patrolled these waters were familiar with all of the commercial fishing boats. It was customary to be boarded several times a year, an annoyance for the honest fisherman to be stopped in the middle of the heated work.

They were interested in more than just keeping lobster men from doing damage to each other. There was a strict size limit on crawfish. Possession of even one under-sized lobster, or a female with eggs, could bring a heavy fine, or loss of a license, impossible to replace, marking the end of a career.

Close to the inshore islands, there were more small lobster than legal size. It was a consistent area that guaranteed the traps would always fill up with what they called "shorts" or "monkeys." There was a thriving black market willing to pay good cash for the delicious morsels. It was part of the adventure for many to sneak in a few bags of small lobster tails and collect a substantial bonus for the day.

Aubrey, one of the young captains, openly bragged about the hundreds of pounds of "monkeys" that he hid deep in the bilge of his boat. It was an oily, tight squeeze to crawl under the deck to find his secret hiding place. He joked that the marine patrol would never mess up their nice clean uniforms to find it. He took delight in tormenting law enforcement, especially Captain Warner, who always put on his broad brimmed hat before he stepped off of his "gray thunder," a formula power boat that was confiscated from smugglers and converted for use by law enforcement. Nothing on the water could out-run him. He struck a no-nonsense image, wearing his hat and resting his hand on his holstered service colt.

There was an obvious ongoing vendetta between the two men.

Captain Warner boarded Aubrey's boat every time he saw him. He knew what the cocky young fisherman was up to. He was frustrated but determined to find the part of the boat where the illegal lobster tails were hidden.

The marine patrol not only had state law to enforce they also had the power to write someone up for federal offenses. The blatant drug smuggling that a few commercial boats were in-volved with was another thing they kept an eye out for. Having a big bust or two under their belt would be the highlights of their career.

Shorty finally had a few perfect days and caught thousands of dollars' worth of crawfish. Hard work and standing up to his own frustration were beginning to pay off.

Or so it seemed.

His gear was poised to do well and he was expecting to salvage the season. His confidence was short lived when, once again, they began to come up empty.

One look at the clean condition of his empty traps, along with a few broken off lobster legs stuck in between the slats, was proof that they were chopper-block full as recently as the day before.

Shorty's teeth clenched and then his neck burned as he began to realize that he'd been robbed. It was hard to accept that another fisherman had taken the liberty to pay themselves with his hard, honest labor, but he wasn't surprised.

It became serious when he pulled the last fifty traps for the week. They had all the signs of once being full of money fish but the thief made it personal when he used a hatchet to break all of the funnels on these expensive new traps. The damage was too much to repair on the boat. Forcing him to bring them back to the dock, to sit useless until they could be rebuilt for the next year.

By the end of the season, he had lost more than half of his gear. A few were consumed by the ocean and her rugged winter weather but most, he suspected, were either stolen or just cut away. A not so friendly welcome from his new rivals probably posing as friends back at the docks. He expected to be tested but not this hard.

Shorty would much rather have a good day than a bad one, but he was unnerved by the challenge. He considered doing some damage of his own, knowing that if he stood down and didn't fight back the problem would only get worse. But he would risk blaming the wrong people, causing them all to turn on him.

When he confided in his wise old friend Sebastian, the

advice was simple. "Don't get mad, get even." He encouraged patience. Something Shorty with his youthful energy was still trying to develop. But he went with the smart advice and continued to quietly take the beating and work with what he had left. With his eyes and ears open he hoped to catch an unusual look or a phony vibe from someone around the docks. Then he would know who to watch. If this was some sort of a cruel initiation it would have to end with his first season. Or else the temptation to lash out would overpower his will to remain at peace.

THE TALL MAN
CAN DO THE WORK

Shorty's favorite part of the day was having coffee with the always positive old fisherman.

If he moved very slowly and carefully, he could now step onto Sebastian's boat without scaring away the wild bird. Pancho was beginning to feel comfortable with another human in his space, but Shorty still had to sit inside the cabin and keep some distance from the wary bird.

The conversations between the men were spirited and covered many different topics. Shorty brought a new joke everyday which usually sounded corny, but the more ridiculous they were the more both men laughed.

Shorty would ask what the Spanish words were for many of the common things around the docks. The names of different types of fish, and so on. Sebastian was quick to become the teacher. He told the young captain to find a Spanish dictionary. From then on, they would only speak in Spanish, forcing the learning to go faster.

At first it was painstakingly slow for Shorty to look up words and try to use sentences that always seemed to be worded backwards. Before long they were able to carry on a few clumsy conversations in the Cuban dialect.

From time to time they found themselves talking about two completely different subjects. Sebastian would ask a question about baseball and Shorty would go on about how much he loved Cuban food. The funny screw-ups caused both men to cut loose and laugh like a couple of kids. Sometimes they would become carried away with the time and Shorty would get a late start to work. Because he wasn't accustomed to being in a cabin that was built for smaller men, Shorty would often jump up quickly, only to bang his head on the low hanging-ceiling rafters. The knock was often hard enough to shake the whole boat.

The old fisherman would act concerned until he was sure the young captain wasn't going to pass out from a serious head injury. Then he would complain about his young friend's hard head doing damage to his old wooden boat. As Shorty rapidly rubbed the sharp pain of another growing knot on his head he would laugh at his own clumsy ways. He couldn't believe how he could forget and make the same mistake so often. He joked with the old fisherman that he would someday shave his head and they could count the permanent dings and dents on his thick skull.

Sebastian enjoyed his time with the tall young captain. He

was different than most of the cocky young men who worked around the docks, one who wasn't afraid to admit that he didn't know it all. He welcomed the honest questions and was happy to share what he knew.

The strong coffee gave Shorty a good boost of energy that would propel him through the labor of the day, at least through the morning.

Shorty considered Sebastian a treasure trove of information. The morning visit with Pancho and Sebastian served him well. It woke up his brain and reinforced his positive attitude. He was grateful to have at least one person in this challenging new life that he could trust.

Day after day, the humor and honest sharing of information formed a bond between the two men. There was a father-to-son feeling in their friendship and that worked for both of them.

Others liked Shorty from the beginning. The owner operators of the marina, Curtis, and his teen aged son saw potential in him and offered up a line of credit if he needed it. They spoke well of him to the other fishermen, helping Shorty to gain more acceptance.

Curtis was a middle-aged man with an old man's back, broken down by a lifetime of picking up too much weight for a living. His son was a chunky kid and as strong as any two adult men. He was always happy and wore round framed glasses with noticeably thick lenses that magnified the size of his eyes.

He appeared to have no neck, presenting a comedic profile that framed his quirky personality. He was another big guy with a funny name. Everyone called the smiley kid "Bigfoot."

They were the hardest working men that Shorty had ever known. Not only did they maintain the docks, they also worked the fish house, providing the fuel, bait and ice for more than fifty boats. They were the middlemen who weighed the fresh seafood from each boat and packed it on ice to be trucked to the distributors in Miami. They still had to find the time to do the administrative work and make sure everyone was paid.

They were from a family who had lived in the Keys for hundreds of years, descended from a famous pirate of history. It seemed natural that they would be working on the water like the other locals. Yet, they didn't want anything to do with "that damn ocean." Neither of them owned a boat. They were proud to call themselves, "land lubbers."

It was coming into the off season and Shorty had to cut his losses. He started right into the land work. Wasting no time, he began repairing what was left of his old traps, building as many new ones as he could over the next four months.

Now that he had a better idea of how to fish these waters the next season promised to be better but he would need to find a decent mate, one that would make his solo effort a team effort. A good first mate could help him stay on top of his gear, making him less vulnerable to the more carnivorous types of competition.

Most of the people who worked at this marina were American fishermen with Welsh last names. They were very clannish, calling themselves "Conchs," and shared a long seafaring history in this part of the world. Descended from privateers, sponge divers, and salvers of shipwrecks. By heritage, they believed the southern waters from Key West to the Dry Tortugas belonged to them. They considered anyone coming from north of Marathon key a "damn Yankee."

There was also a substantial group of Cuban Americans in the mix. They added colorful noise to the marina atmosphere, their loud conversations were animated, and appeared like an aggressive dance. Even their small talk was passionate. Just as they were in each other's face, and seemed like they would break into a fight, they would turn and walk away, laughing at each other.

Although both groups had differences in culture, side by side, for generations, they made their living on the same ocean. Connected by the same labor and dangers, they saw each other as equals.

The young grew up and went to school together, producing many mixed marriages with smart, beautiful, multicultural children, the natural blending proving that "love conquers all."

When any boat from the marina broke down on the ocean, or if anyone was overdue and couldn't be contacted by radio, they would all drop what they were doing and head out to sea. Always willing to take the chance to rescue a fellow fisherman who might someday come to rescue them.

Most of the men that Shorty worked beside were family people. During the off season, or on days that were too rough to go out on the ocean, the boats became a popular place for people to gather. Fathers and sons would work on the walls of traps that were stacked on the lots behind their boats. The mothers and daughters would cook rich, spicy meals of seafood, fresh from the ocean.

Shorty was becoming more of a familiar face. Often, he was waved over to join in with the different families. He considered the boat cooked food to be far better than the expensive meals in the downtown restaurants. It made him feel good to be included.

The Cuban Americans had a special liking for him because he made the attempt to speak in their original language. They encouraged him and were willing to help him find the right words. He was becoming a trusted friend of Sebastian who was one of the elders in their community, and it pleased them that Shorty took the time to look after him.

There was a group of about fifteen younger lobstermen who hung out together. They were mostly single, and closer in age to Shorty but were slowest to thaw to the presence of an outsider. Some were captains and others were mates who worked on the various boats. They were the real professionals of the southern waters, the strong backbones and tough hands that harvested the most lobster.

Fiercely competitive, they pushed each other to pull more

traps and produce more crawfish. Shorty had run into each of them over the last few months. Skunk Ape seemed to have a terminal problem with his hygiene. When he joined with the group, they always gave him plenty of space. He never seemed to understand why he was running everyone off. He was a nice enough guy but a challenge to the fresh air around him. There was Lorenz Slow who moved like a sloth but did everything perfectly. He was always grumpy even when he was happy. Whatever little he would add to the conversation wasn't very well thought out and sounded kind of stupid.

There was no missing Tumble weed and his bushy mangle of beard and hair. He was clownish and once he got started, he talked way too much. But at times he would go completely silent and take on the brooding look of someone with a sharp edge. Tumbleweed was a funny guy but not one to mess with.

And then there was Bruce.

Bruce approached Shorty on day one, pressing for a job. He had a regular route he made around the marina, stopping at certain boats and avoiding others, asking for day work. He was often turned down and shooed away like an annoying pelican.

Shorty was tempted to give him a try because he needed the extra set of hands. But he had a feeling that this was someone he didn't need to get involved with. There was just something false about him so he held off. No one could accuse Bruce of being short on persistence. Almost daily he came by and asked for something. If it wasn't work it would be a beer or a cigarette, as though he needed some sort of payment for the pleasure of his visit.

Shorty was getting uncomfortable having to make excuses and several times he had to walk him off the boat.

He found out from the other fishermen that this guy was slow and clumsy. He was quick to show up waving a cheesy letter from a sleazy lawyer, trying to sue one of the boats that gave him work for fake injuries. Whenever he was fired from another job items around the work area and boat would go missing. Nothing big or expensive but bundles of slats and box-es of nails would just vanish. He was good at stealing and was never caught. That would have been the last draw that would finish his welcome on the property. He was always on the take, a terminal looser who could be vindictive.

Shorty didn't know whether to feel sorry for him or not. He figured that Bruce was just a chronic asshole, an immovable object around the docks.

Bruce could have easily moved on to someplace else and started over or made a better attempt at the job. He was content with his role as the "whipping post" of the marina. In a strange way he thrived on the put downs, almost proud of his lowly image. He accepted the humiliation as his lot in life and was never discouraged enough to not try and join in every conversation that would have him.

Each of the young lobstermen were unique. The one thing they all had in common was their tough guy bravado. They were all full of themselves in their own way. They weren't particularly friendly but Shorty got a kick out of their wide-open behavior. He understood the younger fisherman because he was one.

Anyone who risked their life for a paycheck had a right, an obligation, to squeeze as much living into every moment they could. It was the tough job that carved their sharp personalities.

Shorty was smart about how he handled each of the young brotherhood of lobstermen. If any of them became a little testy he would give them a little space.

On several occasions, he had to show them that he wouldn't back out of his own, that intimidation didn't work with him.

He knew how to play the game.

Most of them quietly watched the new guy and noticed how well he handled the job alone. Rather than wish him failure, like they might have done in the beginning, some of them began rooting for his success. Only too well did they know how unforgiving the work was. Even as part of a crew, with other hands to help, it could seem impossible.

For Shorty to go it alone on a boat big enough for a full crew proved he had guts. The word among them was, "The tall man can do the work." They couldn't deny any respect for his unrelenting determination.

Aubrey, the young captain who enjoyed tormenting law enforcement, was the first of the younger group to stop by and be friendly. He was extraordinarily happy with himself and usually upbeat, snapping his fingers to a song in his head, as he strutted around the marina. He had a loud voice and his smile was a little too big to be real. He approached Shorty often and shared his own brand of humor, usually derogatory and disgusting.

Shorty found him interesting and worth sharing a few laughs with but he noticed Sebastian didn't like Aubrey.

The intuitive old man folded his arms and went silent whenever Aubrey came around. Sebastian glared at him with obvious distrust, as though he could sense the danger behind the overly friendly noise that only Aubrey could make.

Shorty was anxious to fit in with the younger fishermen but he remembered Sebastian's reaction and decided to be a little more cautious with this one.

Aubrey had no problem sharing his personal life with anybody and everybody. He always had some ridiculous story about his divorce and losing custody of his two young daughters and getting into fights with the boyfriends of his ex-wife. Then he would go on and on about the big, bad marine patrol officer who had it in for him, always flinging the most colorful insults toward his nemesis Captain Warner.

Most of that nonsense really didn't concern Shorty. But he would always listen if only for the amusement value.

Aubrey was quick to break out a few lines of what he called the "Peruvian marching powder," cocaine. Shorty would quietly refuse the offer. He didn't want anybody to think he wasn't cool but he was feeling pretty good being sober. He ignored the scramble for the lines on the plate and made himself busy in another direction.

Aubrey had one mate, Chuck, who was the quiet, sensible half of the team. He smiled through his captain's colorful rants. During a pause in the noise, he would offer a few quiet, thoughtful words. Shorty thought Chuck was the most likable guy in this strangely elite group of young fishermen. He seemed to be more trustworthy and less dangerous than the rest.

Shorty heard that a few years back, Chuck had also been an outsider who was from way up north in Maine. Having a great deal of fishing experience in the cold and rough north Atlantic, he migrated south to fish the kinder waters.

Being a true Yankee, he must have had to fight his way into the closed territory of the Conchs. He had to prove himself worthy over and over, until he was accepted on the commercial docks without a challenge.

Chuck wasn't a big guy but he was fast and powerful, very athletic. He took to the work and became one of the better mates at the marina. He could do the work of two men and was paid a double share for it. Aubrey was lucky to have him on board. All he had to do was drive the boat from trap to trap and Chuck could work the deck without a hitch, giving a loyal effort to whatever boat he was on.

As much as Shorty liked the man from Maine, he realized he had a worsening drug problem. Whenever someone would cut up a few lines of cocaine for the offering Chuck would scrape his small portion into the plastic of a cigarette pack and disappear to a quiet place to fire it into his veins. Aubrey would shake his head as he watched his mate leave, as if snorting the drug was somehow superior to the ways of a needle junkie.

Many times, Chuck would walk across the street and hook up with Sunshine from the homeless crew. Shorty assumed they were a couple who languished together whenever there was a little windfall of drugs.

He felt sorry for Chuck. He had more smarts and talent than the rest. It wouldn't be long before the drug would steal his physical power. It looked like some of the veins on his arms were beginning to collapse. Nevertheless, Shorty considered Chuck a friend, and always treated him that way.

Aubrey was the unofficial leader of the young brotherhood of fishermen. He became instrumental in bringing Shorty into the fold. Sometimes, after a long day on the ocean, and always on a payday, the wild young men gathered on Aubrey's boat to start drinking. It took a while before Shorty was encouraged to join them. These were the last group of people to give up the space that he carved out of their life.

There was a bit of intrigue among them. The best way to figure out who was worth knowing or who to keep an eye on was to be among them. Over time, he could measure up each one and would know how to navigate in their world. They were likable to his face but he wondered which of his new buddies ripped him off during the last season.

Whenever he saw Falon, a hot flush passed through his body, preparing his muscles to be ready for anything. The mean-looking man with the long red hair never approached him face to face, but always stopped and glared in his direction.

Falon had a long, grooved scar that ran from his eye to his jaw. It looked like a wound from a bullet graze. His nose was bent and disfigured, broken in a brawl, probably more than once. But it was those beady green eyes that could go right through someone that completed his look of a fighting man.

Shorty would just turn the other way and shake off the threat of a showdown. It was best to ignore him, go about his business. He had to be careful not to show any fear. The slightest weakness would be like an invitation to the most aggressive types.

He did take notice that Falon worked alone. He had a small, beat-up boat and not many traps. Yet, he always seemed to do well at the scales. It was beginning to make sense. Perhaps he was the one who hurt his business. Shorty was almost sure of it.

From time to time, Falon stepped onto the boat with the others. He would help himself to a beer from the cooler, never staying for long and saying little. He enjoyed his ability to intimidate. Everyone would go silent for a moment, someone would offer their seat, a few others would just leave. Shorty wasn't the only one who felt uncomfortable whenever the red-faced man came around.

It was rumored he was mentally ill and someone to avoid. One guy said that he lived in a tent in one of the run-down campgrounds on the northern part of Stock Island. Nobody had ever seen him downtown or anywhere but the docks.

Aubrey would break the awkward silence with an off-color joke. Then the brotherhood would resume their rambunctious party.

The beers that were chugged on the boat would become more beers that were chugged downtown. Key West was a party town and bar hopping was a favorite pastime for the wild young men of commercial fishing.

Though Shorty was surrounded by heavy drinking it held no temptation to fall off of the wagon. It was more fun to have a clear head and watch everyone else become more drunk and act crazier as the night wore on. He was the responsible one, sometimes talking them out of trouble when they were rowdy enough to get kicked out of a bar. He was often the provider of a safe ride home.

The next day, when they were sober, he might have to take them back down town and help them remember where they parked their vehicles. It was their idea of a good night to be drunk enough to lose their own cars.

The brotherhood of young lobstermen called the down town district, "The meat rack." There were plenty of pretty girls on vacation packed in the clubs and bars, often interested in meeting one of the locals. These were young, unattached men and they were the locals. Getting laid was another way to compete with each other, the fun way.

Shorty was different from the rest, unashamed to be a little more romantic and not willing to treat any lady like a one-night convenience. It was seeing what his mom went through when he was too young to protect her from men who promised the moon and stars only to be gone the next morning.

He talked to quite a few pretty girls who were interesting but they were only there for a few days and lived in faraway states. Knowing how his own heart worked he thought that if he let himself get too close, he might become attached and set himself up for another disappointment. Long-distance relationships never worked. The other guys teased him about being so picky and honorable in his quest to find "Miss Right."

For a young man who hung with a tough guy crowd Shorty had no qualms about taking the moral high ground. He kept to his ways. If they gave him too much guff, he warned them about catching something even Ajax wouldn't be able to scrub off. Indeed, some of them missed a day's work to stand in line at the clinic for a shot to cure a sexually transmitted disease. A.I.D.S. was just beginning to become a worry in places like Key West.

Shorty truly believed he would someday find the perfect lady and make a family to be proud of. He knew what he wanted. Being a real dad would be his way to make up for not having one of his own.

It was going on the second year since his only real relationship fell apart and he often felt lonely but the pain and confusion was still a fresh memory. It would be worth the wait to get things right the next time. It was his dream to someday turn around and there she would be, standing in the light with the right kind of smile. He had faith that she was out there and he would keep his heart available for that fine day

HOPEFUL POSSIBILITIES

Shorty usually went to his boat around dawn so he could afford a little more time with Sebastian. It was always better to dig into the heaviest work during the cooler part of the day.

A few years back, he managed to let himself become dehydrated and had a heat stroke caused by overdoing it under the southern summer sun. Even for young people in excellent shape it was no fun and it took a while to recover. Another lesson he learned the hard way.

He saw his friend Sebastian standing on the dock tossing his cast net. The old rusty bucket was over flowing with thread herring.

Throwing the net was something Shorty had tried many times over the years. He just couldn't find the knack for it. With every cast he made, the net would hit the water shaped more like a banana than a proper circle. If he caught any fish at all it was by accident.

It was a skill he wanted to add to his tool belt so he asked the old fisherman to give him a few pointers. Sebastian was always ready to help his young friend, so he showed him how to fold the net and hold it the right way to spin a good cast.

Shorty paid close attention but every time he tried; it just wouldn't open up. The net would plop, oblong, into the water, and scare away the bait fish. When he tried to toss it a bit farther, it opened better but he didn't pull it in quickly enough, and it became hung up on some kind of debris on the bottom.

Sebastian told the young captain not to worry. He went to his boat and came back with a diving mask and an odd-looking flat bone needle wrapped with clear line. He handed over the mask with a smile.

Shorty went for a swim.

He dove in to avoid the sharp barnacles and razor oysters that grew on the pilings at the water line. The net was wrapped around an old engine block, and it took a good while to free it without adding to the damage. Shorty handed up the torn net to Sebastian. Then he looked for a place to climb out of the murky harbor water without being cut. He grabbed one of the old frayed ropes still tied to the dock. Out of the corner of his eye he saw a bright red flash of color next to the fish house. He turned his head and saw a young lady get out of a shiny new car.

It wasn't typical to see someone so well-dressed around the docks. Most everyone wore work clothes. She looked more like a professional person, perhaps from an urban area somewhere.

With a briefcase in hand, she walked over to the small office built on to the side of the fish house.

Shorty couldn't help but notice the long, blond hair that reached her waist, swaying back and forth as she moved. It looked nice as it brushed against her tan arms. From this angle, he couldn't see her face. Half way out of the water, he hung on the rope, mesmerized with the way she walked.

He shrugged his shoulders and thought she must be a buyer or someone involved with the seafood business. She looked way too classy to have any interest in a grungy fisherman.

Even Sebastian looked her way and smiled. Then he looked down and saw that Shorty was gawking like a fool at the young lady. His smile disappeared. Instead of extending a hand to help Shorty out of the water he backed up, showing a little anger toward his young friend.

Shorty stood on the dock soaking wet and taken back by the look on Sebastian's face. He had never seen him mad and had no idea what he might have done wrong. Sebastian impatiently demonstrated how to make a few difficult knots with the bone needle. He tossed the torn net at Shorty and said to "fix it." He showed his back to the young captain and walked away.

Shorty was dumbfounded with the quick change of attitude in his friend. He had already insisted on buying a new net or fix the old one. Sebastian was the last person on earth he wanted to be on the outs with.

It didn't seem like the torn net was the issue. There was

something else going on. He caught up to the old fisherman and stopped him. Then he forcefully asked what the problem was.

Sebastian turned a stern face to the young captain and laid down a barrage of Spanish before he stepped on to his boat.

Completely flabbergasted, Shorty filtered through the words to find the meaning. He came up with something about the way he was drooling over the young lady, "like she was a juicy steak" just waiting to be devoured.

How could he be doing anything wrong by looking at her? He only watched her for a minute. Well, maybe two. She was just so easy on the eyes. He couldn't understand why the old fisherman would even care if he was taking a good look at her.

He sulked over to his boat and spread the net on the deck. On his hands and knees, he began the tedious work of mending the net with complicated knots.

After a few hours he saw the old fisherman walking over his way. His usual soft smile had returned. Sebastian leaned over and quietly said that "the lady" was his granddaughter. Her name was, "Brianna." He gave Shorty a sly smile as he pointed a warning finger at his face as if to say "don't get any big ideas!"

He explained that the dock master Curtis and his son Bigfoot had their hands full with working the scales and loading trucks. They were falling behind on the office work, so they hired Brie to handle their book keeping. Now, she would be the one who signed his paychecks.

For the last four years, she had attended a small college in New England. Now she was home with a degree in accounting. It was a rare opportunity to have a job for her skills come up in this part of the world. He had been worried that she might have to find work in some distant northern city. The position at the fish house opened up and became a perfect fit.

Sebastian was relieved knowing she would be close by and he could see her often, to know she was safe.

Shorty understood why a grandfather would be so protective of his granddaughter, especially around the commercial docks with so many obnoxious men. Shorty sensed that Sebastian was giving a hint of approval of the interest he had in her. He felt comfortable enough to glance back toward the fish house, hoping he might get a better look at Brie who really knew how to walk.

He saw that a cloud of dust was coming through the screen door of the small office. She must have changed her clothes and had a broom in her hands. He noticed that she had managed to pull all of the old file boxes and a heavy safe into the parking lot. She also had a few cans of new paint standing by.

Shorty was impressed with her whirlwind cleaning job on the long-neglected office. He knew how cluttered it was. When he went in to settle his books there wasn't enough room to sit. He wondered how Curtis and Bigfoot could keep their business straight in such a jumbled mess.

The gentleman in him wanted to walk over and offer to help. He was also curious because he still hadn't seen her face.

But he didn't want to appear too forward by pouncing so quickly. He was nervous and not really sure why.

When he stood up to stretch his back from mending the frustrating net. He saw Aubrey strutting at a quick pace behind his boat and towards the office. He was wearing an extra big smile and showing extreme confidence. Normally Aubrey would have stopped to chat but he looked like he was on a mission.

There were a few whistles from some of the men around the marina.

Shorty shook his head and looked back down at the net. He told himself that he was too late. With all of this attention from around the docks any attempt to meet her now would feel awkward.

Back to his knees, he continued repairing the cast-net and, from time to time, looking over her way.

Aubrey was hovering around her like an overly-friendly pest. Her body language showed she was politely annoyed with his distractions and was trying to work around him.

Late in the afternoon Shorty decided to finish the net the next day. He folded it into the old rusty bucket and placed it on the stern of Sebastian's boat. One last time, he glanced towards the office and saw that the red car was gone.

Just then, Brie pulled up behind Sebastian's boat.

The old fisherman stood on the dock with a big smile and his opened arms.

When Shorty finally saw her face, he quickly concluded that

she was way out of his league. The Hispanic side of her family had given her the supple olive skin that tans so deeply. It set off the luminescence in her sky-blue eyes. Her fine features didn't need any makeup and were framed by her long, light brown hair with golden highlights kissed by the sun.

Tingles and pleasant rushes ran from his neck to his fingertips. Shorty was smitten.

Rising up through the sugar-sweet music in his head came that familiar inner voice. This time he listened a little closer and clearly heard the words, "Take a good look. You might see that beautiful face for the rest of your days."

It was the nicest thought he ever had.

Was this rarely heard voice in his head for real, or was it just wishful thinking? Could it be the whisper of a friendly angel giving him a mystical glimpse into the future?

Finding clever things to say was never an issue for Shorty but when she stepped onto her grandfather's boat and glanced his way his brain took a wobble. He almost wished she would ignore him long enough to gather his nerve and come up with something to say, something that wouldn't sound clumsy or weird.

He noticed that Pancho was strangely undisturbed when she went on the boat. He wondered why the wild bird didn't take to the air with someone unfamiliar, coming so close. Then he thought that perhaps there was some sort of instinct that allowed the bird to know which humans were safe to be around. Maybe Pancho didn't mind humans as long as they were pretty girls.

Sebastian and his beautiful granddaughter began talking in rapid-fire Spanish. It had been a while since they had spent much time together. They were catching up on matters concerning the family. Shorty pretended to be busy on his boat. He made no attempt to understand the conversation that belonged only to them.

Besides, they were talking so fast he couldn't keep up with the translation.

Sebastian looked over his way and, in English, he said that he had someone he wanted her to meet. He reminded his granddaughter that he had mentioned the young captain in some of their monthly letters.

As they were walking over Shorty noticed that she had the same soft smile as her grandfather. It was a smile of contentment, an unwavering love of life.

Sebastian introduced the two young people. Brie had a little fun with Shorty's name, no differently than her grandfather had when first meeting the tall young captain. She cocked her head a little to one side and slowly rolled her eyes up to his. In a musical voice she asked him how tall he was?

This woke Shorty out of his enchantment enough to try and make a joke. She wasn't the first lady he met who had that same opening question. He scratched his head like he was trying to remember. He said that "the last time I checked, nine foot six and a half inches."

Being tall was mostly a blessing, only occasionally a curse.

He never minded having a little fun at his own expense. It was only natural for him to show a little humility.

He reached for her small soft hand and gave her a firm handshake, offering his services if she ever needed a ladder.

She held the young captain's gaze while she smiled at his goofy comments. For a few seconds, her eyes shined into his. She gave his hand a little extra squeeze before letting go.

Brie left the boat and went to her car. She carried back a box of goodies that her mother had made for her grandfather. She told Sebastian, loud enough for Shorty to hear, that she would have to have a carpenter raise the doorway to the office. She looked toward Shorty, and in a teasing way, said she wouldn't want some "big guy" to bang their head on payday.

Immediately, Shorty thought that Sebastian must have told her about his embarrassing habit of banging the top of his head, but realized she was playing with him. She might have shown no interest at all and just ignored him. But she didn't.

That evening, he walked home with his head filled with hopeful possibilities.

These wonderful new feelings were interrupted by a few insecurities. A lady of her qualities must already be in a relationship, probably with someone better looking and better educated, someone with potential to be more than a fisherman.

He had forgotten to see if she was wearing a ring.

He decided that because she was Sebastian's granddaughter, she might be the type to follow her heart. Maybe he had a chance, after all.

Sebastian lit up his evening pipe and sat on his cooler waiting for the sunset. He noticed that Pancho was still on the boat. He couldn't remember when the big beautiful bird stayed around for the whole day.

He had nine grandchildren and over the years he told each one that they were his favorite, but Brie was the one he was really closest to. She was his youngest. Her father had been killed in Vietnam when she was just a young girl. Sebastian moved in with his daughter to help raise Brie. He searched the past and remembered her father to be someone he really liked. He had sandy hair and a botched but corny sense of humor. He realized that his friend Shorty reminded him a lot of him. Perhaps that's why he took to the young captain from the beginning.

He had been a little unnerved with the way Shorty was looking at his pretty granddaughter. She was fiercely independent. He worried she might wind up with some wild young fisherman, one that might take advantage of her good heart or wind up being abusive. But after thinking about it, he believed that this particular wild young fisherman would probably make her happiness the center of his life. The obvious chemistry between the two young people was impossible to ignore. His instincts began to chime in, and he listened for his inner voice. He heard no discernible words but was given a comfortable vision of the two young faces blending into one.

Pancho left the boat at first dark.

Before the old fisherman climbed down to his bunk, he took a plastic container and filled it with some left-over lobster chowder. He wrapped it in a lunch bag and taped it shut. Rather than putting it in the cooler he placed it on top of the piling next to his boat, an offering for a hungry little bird that will sometimes come in the night.

He opened the hatch to sleep in the breeze that cools across the water. It was an easy sleep, knowing his granddaughter was finally home.

WHERE EVIL AND INNOCENCE COLLIDE

A few years back, some of the boats had been broken into and had their electronics stolen. The fishermen themselves found the thief trying to sell the goods at a pawn shop. They took matters into their own hands in the parking lot. It sent a message to those who might consider the commercial boats an easy mark. Even with the gate left open at night, the street people were afraid to enter the marina.

At the far end of the commercial docks the security fence came to an end against the big boulders that formed the jetty. On the other side, there was a sliver of land with a few cabbage palms and clumps of sand spurs, home to some rusted barrels and several broken and abandoned boat hulls. It was probably the only small space on Stock Island that was unseen and never walked on, a good place to be invisible and go unmolested during the night.

For a few months it was home, a place where the child with

the thatch of white hair could hide with enough confidence to actually rest, careful not to go there until after dark, always afraid of losing the secret place to someone else. The child was especially afraid of the foul man they called Bruce. He was always stalking the harbor.

Because it was a tight squeeze through the fence it would be the last place Bruce would look. He was the only one who knew that the child with white hair was really a girl.

Her given name was Ava Loraine. She learned the hard way that a being a boy attracted a little less attention from some of the demented who troll the homeless world. Ava was born without a tiny piece of her brain, the part that connects and allows communication between both sides. Simply put, she had a split brain.

The challenge became her miracle. Over time she somehow managed to reroute her thoughts helping her to be very high functioning, considering the severity of her disability. Out of necessity she developed an extreme level of persistence. It was embedded into her personality and the reason for her survival.

Thinking comes easily and almost automatically to most, but Ava had to manually move each and every thought, leaving her exhausted and discombobulated by the end of every day.

Because of the relentless mental workout her mind became super strong. She had become a savant, having very high skill levels, in a few narrow areas of intelligence. She was an unnoticed and undiscovered genius in music and art. Although she was slow and had a terrible time communicating, whenever she dug deep to find things in her memory, everything she knew would be there etched in her mind like a clear photograph.

As a toddler she was tossed into the system by parents who were too self-absorbed to spare the effort it takes to raise a child with special needs. Passed from place to place, she missed out on any therapy that could have improved her chances. Twice she had run away from the same abusive foster home. To her, living out in the weather and scavenging for nourishment was safer and better than any of the places she had lived.

Along with trouble making up her mind there were a few other traits that weakened her ability to stay alive. She couldn't interpret the intentions of people. Deception was a concept that she couldn't understand. Those few minutes with the nice captain had been confusing to her. Seeing smiles on people usually meant that she was being tricked into another bad situation. Purely innocent, she was always an easy victim. Ava was the most vulnerable of all.

Earlier that evening she heard Bruce with his muddy voice on the other side of the fence. So, she waited in a dark corner of the dog track building until she knew that he was gone before she dared to go near her secret place. In the past, he found her when she thought she was alone. He was fast enough to catch her, and hold her down.

While he rubbed his filthy body on her, and exhaled his garbage breath on her face, she would try to fight back. He would put his fingers on her throat, and stop her from breathing, until he was finished. Ava would pass out from a seizure, a cruel form of mercy, allowing her to come to after the extreme damage was done.

Under one of the overturned boat hulls Ava took a palm frond and made a sweep for any scorpions and other biting creatures.

This was home.

There was a small patch of sand on the point of the jetty where she could see to the end of the channel, and a good way out into the ocean. The smell of the fresh breeze and the sound of the gentle waves were soothing to her unsettled mind. She watched the pretty red and green running lights on the occasional boats coming in or going out of the inlet.

She had her own names for many of the stars in the sky.

Sometimes she would think about the god-like young captain who once gave her a sandwich. Whenever she saw him, she would stop and stare until he noticed her, then quickly run away. Those few minutes of genuine concern had a big impact on her.

One of the best reasons for living here was that it came with a late-night gift of food from a kindly old fisherman who lived on the other side of the marina, next to the nice Captain's big boat. That small part of the world, next to the fish house, felt safe to her. But knowing the marina property was off-limits she was always nervous about going near.

Waiting until the early hours of the morning when the harbor was asleep, and her stomach was hollow and growling, for nourishment. She would become one with the darkness, and moved unseen behind the walls of lobster traps. Once there, she could grab the nice package left on the piling and quickly run back the way she came.

But on this night, while she was softly humming the unwritten music that calmed her mind, she saw something that seemed different out on the water.

As a cloud passed by the quarter moon the blackness opened up with enough light to see beyond the first channel marker offshore. There, she focused on two boats drifting side by side. She recognized one of the lobster boats, one that docked on the other side of the fence from where she hid. She didn't like the way the captain of that boat tossed his trash over the vine covered fence onto her little bit of land.

A few months before Aubrey had noticed her over by the sandwich shop. He sneered an intimidating smile at her and she wasn't sure if it was the bad kind of smile or not. But whenever she saw him after that she became flushed with fear and would quickly look for a shadow to hide behind.

She also knew the fast gray boat and recognized the outline of the policeman with the broad-brimmed hat. She was especially afraid of law enforcement. In the past, they took her back to the same foster home that she ran away from. Where she was locked in a dark bathroom for long periods of time with no light, no sounds, and only conscious of her painful parts.

She tried to think of why the two boats were sitting still and didn't have their pretty lights on. A few square white packages were being passed to the scary looking policeman on the fast gray boat. She believed that they were only exchanging food, or supplies.

The roar of the three big outboards on the policeman's boat startled her back under the cover of the hull.

Captain Warner grabbed his hat and took off at full throttle. He disappeared into the dark ocean before he turned his running lights back on. As the lobster boat idled into the basin, she pinched her nose to stop the burn from the acetone smell of raw cocaine. There were more of the white packages inside the cabin.

After Aubrey's boat backed into his slip and tied off, she braved leaving her broken boat shelter and crawled over to the fence. In perfect silence she curled around a shadow and watched.

Two fancy custom vans backed in behind the lobster boat. She saw four dark men make a line and pass the stinky white packages from the boat to the back doors of the vehicles. They quietly spoke words she didn't understand.

As still as a rock, she only moved her eyes. They were drawn to a small light coming on at the front of the marina. The kindly old fisherman had awakened.

It was getting close to the time of night when she would take the food.

She believed the reason he put out the meal before he went below to sleep was because he didn't want to see her, but didn't mind her stealing the generous meal. Now that he was awake, she wouldn't dare go near. Maybe tonight she would have to be hungry.

The men around Aubrey's boat were careful not to make any noise. They were sneaky about whatever work they were doing. Then, without putting on their lights, they slowly drove out of the marina. Ava turned her head to better hear the grumbling of some mean words from the scary captain, bad ones that she had heard often in her life. Aubrey was on fire with anger. He muffled his cuss words to keep with the silence. He, too, noticed the light go on in Sebastian's boat. When he saw the old man looking his way, he was quick to made another deadly decision.

Stealth was crucial for the bold move of smuggling a big load of cocaine into a crowded marina under everyone's noses. But it was the least expected way of getting the drugs through. The Coast Guard, and other levels of law enforcement, were usually patrolling the remote islands and waterways, the more sensible places to watch for illegal activities. During the nighttime hours the Marine Patrol was the only branch that covered the waters and ports near populated areas.

The way to assure success would be a payoff, either in cash or a portion of the expensive drugs. A crooked cop was a rare asset to have in the drug business. The vendetta between Captain Warner and Aubrey was just theater to distract from the dirty business they did together.

Aubrey's mate, Chuck, had begun to think the war between the two captains seemed a little much. The boat was boarded often but rarely ever searched. The way they had fun with it made him feel like it was a bit of a show.

Earlier that night, when Aubrey had arrived at his boat to take his little jaunt offshore, he found Chuck and Bruce drinking beer in the work area, close by. He was furious. He had told his mate to take a few days off and even gave him an advance on his pay to go have some fun downtown.

Aubrey was very calculating, especially when he was about to break the law. Running into these men on this night, of all nights, was a shock to his plan. He didn't expect to see anyone.

He went over to his mate, readying his fists for an angry explosion but quickly changed to a big smile. His anger would only draw more suspicion to what he was doing here in the off hours. He told Chuck and Bruce to wait while he went below for a few minutes. He had been selling grams of coke to guys like this for years. Perhaps it was time for a friendly little gift, one that would paint them out of the picture for good.

Chuck knew right away that something serious was going down. He didn't want to know anything about it. It sent shivers up his spine. He wanted to get the hell out of there.

Aubrey came back topside and handed his mate an eight ball (one eighth an ounce of cocaine), and said "no charge." He told Chuck to get lost and forget about coming back to work for a few days.

He glared a strange look at Bruce, as if foreseeing his doom. The coke was the perfect distraction for a couple of addicts.

There could be no witnesses during a crime that involved so much dark money. This was his biggest load yet. If Aubrey were to get caught, he would spend the last half of his life in a box with bars, sleeping and eating with the monster-minded inmates of a federal penitentiary. Even in prison, he wouldn't be beyond the reach of the cartel who would hold him responsible for the millions of dollars he stood to lose, an impossible amount that could only be reimbursed in blood.

An unlucky witness, someone in the wrong place at the wrong time, could jeopardize the whole deal. They would have to disappear or be silenced, in one form or another. A quickly forgotten part of the job.

Cocaine comes in its purest form during the first leg of its journey. Too strong for the needle junkies, it would be a life-threatening rush beginning with fire in the veins, and followed by unrelenting convulsions.

They would never have access to the purest cocaine, anyway.

After it reached American shores, it went through a few more hands before reaching street users. Each time, it was cut in half with a benign white power, doubling the profit, through each level of distribution and dealers.

By the time someone injected the drug it was only ten to twenty percent of the original strength, enough to keep them coming back for more, but not strong enough to kill them, creating a steady customer who would linger in dependence for years.

Aubrey had a sample of the uncut, flaky rocks down below. When he made the bag for Chuck and Bruce, he knew it would look like an addict's dream come true. He also knew the purity would be a shock to their system and probably kill them.

No great loss in his mind. This was the big one. He was planning on taking his fortune and getting as far away from the work of fishing and his life on Stock Island as he could. He was looking forward to enjoying a fat, early retirement in some exotic foreign land.

People deep in the business of drugs would sometimes use what they called a "hot shot" to rid themselves of a problem. It was a clean murder, when someone was duped into killing themselves.

For a man like, Aubrey there was no conscience, only annoyance with the curveball his mate and the mooch Bruce tossed him. A worry he didn't need on a nervous night. He added a sprinkle of cyanide crystals from a can of rat poison to make damn sure the job was done. It blended well with the pure rocky cocaine.

Chuck walked away with a strange suspicion about the generous gift, but temptation grew and became stronger than his reasoning. He didn't look back when Aubrey started up his boat and left the marina. He wanted nothing to do with what he suspected was going on.

Bruce's eyes lit up when he saw the drugs. He followed Chuck so closely that he stepped on his heals. He was impossible to lose when there was anything around that would get him high.

Later, after the vans pulled out of the marina and the dangerous deal was on its way to being a success, Aubrey turned his attention to another unexpected witness. He jumped to the dock walking towards the front of the marina. He had something long and heavy in his hand.

He didn't stay on the marina road under the street lights but instead slipped behind the traps and along the inside of the fence. It was the same invisible route that Ava always used.

Still watching from the dark side of the fence it came to her that it was a good thing she had waited. Running into this man, alone and at night, was the thing she feared the most. In her innocence, she thought he was going to talk with the kindly old fisherman.

Maybe later in the night, the old fisherman would go back to sleep and give her another chance at a good meal before the daylight came, and the arrival of people going to work would keep her away.

But the two men didn't seem to be talking. She stood to better see across the water. She began to develop a knot at the base of her throat. This always happened right before something painful was about to happen, either to her or someone else. No stranger to violence she would usually just run away until her legs were too tired to carry her anymore. This time, she was frozen still.

She stood up, straining to see what was happening to the nice old fisherman. Her fingers clutched the fence. and with a weak, congested voice she forced out the unheard words. "Stop. st-st Stop."

She heard a crash that sounded like a car running into the chain link fence followed by two loud gun shots which sent her stumbling backward. She slid and rolled under the old boat hull, breathing fast, shivering, and overwhelmed with fear, afraid the violence would find her. With her struggle to make quick decisions she wasn't sure if she should leave her secret place. It no longer made her feel safe. She didn't want to leave but Aubrey was dangerous and his boat was too close.

Just before daybreak, she crept away, saying goodbye to the best home she had ever known.

THE LOVING FATHER OF THREE YOUNG CHILDREN

In the earliest hours of the morning, Sebastian opened his eyes to the muffled, motoring noise of a crawfish boat. He knew by the sound that it was riding low in the water from carrying a heavy load.

He was annoyed because it was an interruption to some really fine dreaming. Not the usual confusing bits and pieces of nonsensical events. They were clear, accurate flashes of his past, like home movies playing in his mind. It was a pleasant review of long forgotten happiness and exciting adventures. He tried to ignore the unusual activity and go back to sleep, hoping to pick up where he left off in his dream life.

The only one in the marina after hours, Sebastian considered himself the unofficial security guard. By keeping an eye on the property, he felt like he was repaying the kindness of the dock master for letting him live there. The pay phone at the fish house was close by. He kept a can of loose change next to his bed in case he needed to call police. There had never been anything serious enough to have him make that call.

When he got up and dressed, he heard the wheels of several vehicles go past. Then he caught the scent of raw cocaine that wafted over the water, and across his boat. It raised the hair on the back of his neck.

This was more serious than he could handle alone. He thought about turning off his light and closing his cabin door, hoping those dangerous types would leave without noticing him.

But as he sat on the edge of his bunk, he had a vision of his youngest son who died a slow death on this drug. Although the knockout punch of losing a child happened more than five years ago, the sadness still lingered. A day hasn't gone by without regrets and desperate bouts of guilt. He would always feel like he could have done more to save him. Maybe now, he had a chance to save someone else's kid, by preventing this load from hitting the streets.

Against his own screaming instincts, he stepped up on the deck and looked across the water towards the back side of the marina. Standing in the shadows, believing he was unseen, Sebastian watched long enough to be sure of who was involved. When the vans began to leave, he slipped back in his cabin and reached under his bunk, pulling out an old revolver. It was rusted from years of salty air.

Sebastian had no memory of the last time it was fired. The nervous but determined old fisherman's hands rattled as he fumbled with the faded old box of ammo.

The payphone was attached to the fish house under a street light, a few hundred feet away. He would be taking a big risk of being seen but felt like he had already been seen. There was no choice. He needed the police for his own protection.

Perched on the roof of the dog track, behind an air conditioning unit. Falon watched the marina through a night-vision-scope. Close at hand was a listening device picking up whispers, despite the distance. Dressed in dark fatigues, Falon felt confident no one could see, or ever suspect, his surveillance from above.

The mean-faced man with the long red hair was an undercover Federal Marshal, one with a long career of braving the front lines of the war on cocaine. He was positioned for the biggest risk of violence and owned the scars to prove it.

Super Cops were highly trained specialists, with hard experience behind them. Like actors, they took on a persona and played the part for long periods of time. They could be a bartender or a boat mechanic. Some were adept enough to blend in with the addicts and prostitutes. Embedded in the everyday life of high traffic areas for the drug trade, they were the invisible eyes and ears of law enforcement, gathering the information to build investigations and becoming the spearhead for every major bust.

Falon's choice to play an intimidating character had worked perfectly for almost two years. Being an unapproachable man of few words gave him freedom of movement around the commercial docks with very little interaction, lowering the risk of blowing his cover. No one could have guessed that this filthy mad man had a beautiful home on Marathon Key, and a strong but worried wife, always waiting and praying for his safe return.

No one would have believed that such a dangerous looking man would be the tender, loving father of three young children.

The accumulation of information combined with his instincts, led him to alert the task force downtown to coordinate the different levels of law enforcement. It was crucial to ambush the drug deal, and capture the smugglers red-handed. It had to be done right for all of the criminal charges to hold up in court. There also had to be consideration for the safety of any innocent by standers. Arrests on this level were always dangerous. High stakes made desperate men into deadly men.

Earlier that night, Falon had watched, and listened to Aubrey kick Chuck and Bruce out of the marina. When they disappeared in the alleyway behind the sandwich shop, he had a slight sense of relief knowing that he wouldn't have to arrest either one of them.

Falon saw Chuck as a decent man, losing a battle with addiction, and not inclined to become mixed up with the high-level crime about to occur. He wasn't surprised to see Bruce tagging along. He hoped they wouldn't come back and get in the way.

His adrenaline flowed as he watched Aubrey's boat disappear into the night. It would be a while, but his training helped him control the energy and keep it in reserve for the right moment. His mind was sharp. His senses were tuned in. He was in the zone.

Typically, a courier boat from the Keys or the Bahamas would jog offshore and meet with a mother ship, usually a freighter out in the shipping lanes, often with origins in Columbia and carrying a questionable registration from an African country. A quick trip to off-load the drugs, and return before daylight, was the general pattern. If everything went the way that law enforcement expected it would be several hours before Aubrey's boat would return, with a substantial load of illegal contraband.

Falon would video the unloading of the drugs, allowing whatever vehicles were used to leave the gate of the fish house. Then, on his call, the state police would converge on the entrance ramp for A1A north, setting up a quick roadblock, the only way in, or out, of the Keys. County sheriff's deputies would be poised to flank the drivers, and cut them off from behind.

The men in the vans would be higher up in the cartel, bad men with big guns. With few citizens nearby, this was the best place on Stock Island to apprehend them.

Falon would leave his perch and use a drainage ditch to crawl under the chain link fence to arrest Aubrey. The city police would then enter the fish house, and provide him with back up.

For reasons only his superiors knew, the state marine patrol wasn't included in the coalition. Falon was curious about what that reason would be. He could have used their support from the water. There was always a chance that the events could lead into a boat pursuit.

As his mind was doing a rapid-fire review of all the different directions that things could go, a suspicious wave rolled through his mind. He made a mental note to ask Internal Affairs about it.

When the suspect boat left, he put in for a Coast Guard cutter to patrol the shipping lanes out front. The Straits of Florida were vast, and the chances slim that they would find the right ship for a search and seizure. Despite all the effort and planning to make the arrests on land, it would be a preferred piece of luck for them to apprehend the mother ship, and the courier boat, out on the water. This would land the biggest catch of drugs, and possibly multiple levels of the cartel. Most importantly, it would keep the potential violence away from a populated area where innocent bystanders could find themselves in the crossfire.

After four hours of hawking the marina and the surrounding area, Falon did a few stretches to loosen up, making sure his body could react when the time came to make his move.

The roar of three big outboards taking off in the distance made him jump back on his scope. Looking out into the dark ocean toward the last channel marker, he managed to catch a glimpse of a rooster-tail wake behind a cigarette racing boat.

He snapped a few thermal images of the familiar vessel. They would need to be processed later.

Falon's temples throbbed in sync with his heartbeat as he focused on Aubrey's boat casually reentering the harbor.

Then he caught some movement, just on the other side of the fence from where the drug laden boat would dock. Suspecting it was one of the homeless who had inadvertently come too close to the wrong place at the worst possible time, he was forced to consider the safety of a citizen during a dicey arrest. He could only hope whoever it was, would leave the area, or hide, before things went down.

He heard the noise of tires on the marina road. He turned to watch two high-end custom vans with their lights off pull in behind where Aubrey had just docked.

This was the moment that he had worked long and hard to reach. He weaponized the powerful energy of his fears and took the lead of the surprise attack.

He spoke clearly into his radio to "cast the net." Everyone involved took their well-coordinated positions. Just after the call, his eyes were drawn to a small light coming on in one of the small boats near the fish house.

When he saw the old fisherman come out on his deck, he realized he had two innocents to factor into the evolving plan. One on each side of the on-going crime.

The interception was too far along to call it off, so his timing would have to be perfect. Falon smoothed his nerves and remained steady behind his recording equipment.

After the drugs were loaded in to the vans and they exited the marina, he rappelled down from the roof, and into the parking lot of the dog track.

From the ground it was difficult to see through the chain link fence, but he still had eyes on Aubrey, who was nervously cleaning his boat.

Swift and unseen, he reached the drainage ditch and suddenly his prey disappeared from view

The only thing he could do was listen. He realized his worst fear when he heard running footsteps in the direction of the fish house. This quickly changed his mission, from making the well-planned arrest, to protecting an innocent life.

He had hoped the old fisherman would ignore what was going on and go back to sleep. But it made sense that he'd try to reach the payphone, and report the suspicious activity.

He caught a glimpse of Aubrey, moving fast with something in his hand. It looked like a pipe. He was still too far away to stop whatever was coming.

In a dead run, and still on the wrong side of the fence, Falon could only be a helpless witness to the vicious assault. He heard the distant snap of breaking bone, and winced through the steam of his breath. He thought he saw a pistol fly from Sebastian's hand.

Aubrey landed a few more powerful swings of the lead filled pipe and the feisty old fisherman went down.

It was too late to make it around to the gate. When Falon reached the area nearest to Sebastian's boat, he roared a rebel yell, his last hope of distracting Aubrey away from the old fisherman. His training kicked in as he hit the tall chain link fence and breached the razor wire like it wasn't there.

When Falon landed, he wobbled his balance for only a half a second. It was long enough to hinder the draw of his own sidearm. Still, he charged right into the old pistol that was now in Aubrey's hand.

This time the rusted old gun, with outdated ammo, fired twice.

Aubrey was standing wild in a halo of his own flames, fueled by consuming a large amount of the drug he was smuggling, and now stoked by the blood lust.

Some people can remain lucid during a heightened state. He managed to find a rag and wipe his fingerprints from the old gun. He carefully placed it next to Sebastian's hand. But he was completely taken off guard and confused about the sudden appearance of Falon.

The noise of gunfire was the one thing he meant to avoid. That's why he'd chosen the more silent, more intimate, method of eliminating the unlucky witness.

With a strangely satisfied smile, he skipped over the bodies, and onto the dock.

Just as he believed his crimes were a success and his fortune secure, his head was jerked around by flashing blue lights bouncing off of the bottom of some low-lying clouds.

They lit up the entire east side of the island.

In an instant, his adrenaline switched its flow away from his blood lust and began to fuel his rattling fear. Such a massive amount of law enforcement could only mean one thing.

He had just lost more than a ton of Peruvian pink-flake cocaine, worth tens of millions of dollars. This would directly connect him to the murders.

Like a silent demon, he ran across the dark parking lots, and through back yards. Other than the barking of a dog, and the panting of his swift shadow. He fled the scene unnoticed.

THE FATHER HE
NEVER KNEW

Shorty was a morning person because he usually slept like a
rock. No sooner than his head would hit the pillow it would be
daylight again. But that night he was restless and had disturbing dreams, nothing he could remember but unsettling just
the same. He woke up several times with an ominous feeling,
sensing that something was wrong.

He considered getting dressed and checking on his boat. In
his drowsy state it was easy to convince himself to roll over and
go back to sleep. His boat was his only worry and he was sure
that Sebastian would jump on the pay phone and call him if
anything was wrong.

He took his time rolling out of bed because his only plan for
the day was to spend some time downtown running errands.
Perhaps he would find an empty bench on Duval Street and do
some people watching, always fun in a place like Key West.

It was the weekend so the fish house office would be closed.

There was no reason to come up with an excuse to check on his boat because the beautiful lady who had just walked into his life wouldn't be at the docks until Monday.

As he met the morning, he noticed the air felt thick and heavy. He checked the air conditioning and it was blowing cold air. It was a slight, but strange sort of feeling. He was a little annoyed because it seemed to be trying to spoil his day. When he locked the door behind him, he was startled by a screaming ambulance coming from the direction of the marina.

He ran down the steps and into the parking lot to get a better look. He gasped seeing the red and blue flashing lights between the fish house and his boat. A hot rush exploded below his chest and above his stomach. He felt weightless as he hit the ground in a blind run.

Then he was stopped short, by the loud blast of a truck horn and the siren of a second ambulance that came so close to hitting him. He stumbled backwards, just missing the wheels.

He rounded the corner through the marina gate, dodging the gathering crowd and a line of police vehicles, manhandling people who were in his way.

When he saw the yellow crime tape on Sebastian's boat his legs went heavy. It felt like he was trying to run through water. Everything around him fell into slow motion. All sounds became deep with quiet echoes.

As the tragic reality closed in. He begged the universe to have mercy on his friend.

Long moments passed before he could force his legs to carry him any closer. Paralyzed by fear, he was terrified to look and see what kind of darkness had taken his bright spot in the world.

He forced himself to push forward through the cars, and people. He noticed some of the fishermen with their arms crossed. They were looking at the ground and shaking their heads. Then he saw Bigfoot, with his tender heart, sitting on the stern of his boat, openly crying.

As he reached the yellow tape that surrounded Sebastian's boat, the noise became more muffled and everything around him faded away. He had to blink his dry eyes a few times to find his focus. He could make out a large puddle of fresh blood on the deck space just outside the cabin. There were smear marks beginning to dry around the edges. Lying close by, an old pistol.

A single sound penetrated the mumbling noise around him. One of the officers said Sebastian's name followed by the word "Deceased." That word went through him like a knife.

Shorty stood, shaking his head, repeating, "No. No. No."

He held up his fist, looked up to the sky challenging God and his so-called plan for us. Why did it always seem like good things happened to evil people and the worst of what this world has to offer to the best? Sebastian had no enemies. He offended no one. How could he deserve this apparent violent end to his peace-loving life?

When he opened his eyes, there was Pancho circling above the kindly old fisherman's boat. He appeared to be lost and confused.

Shorty felt dizzy and dropped his head to see where the ground was. Stars fired off to both sides of his vision. He looked for a clear place to land or anything to hold onto to before he grayed out. It was a similar feeling to when he lost his finger and had to fight off the shock. Only this time the fade was too strong to battle.

Shock is nature's way of showing us mercy, making us numb during impossible pain, leaving us with blurry memories of those unbearable moments.

The violence of that moment punched Shorty so hard in his heart he stumbled backwards, bumping into a police officer and almost knocking him over. The officer caught his balance and turned to the tall fisherman with aggression. Then he saw that Shorty's eyes were floating as he staggered. The officer quickly realized there was something wrong. He helped him over to a stray lobster trap and made him sit. He offered some water and asked if he needed to see a paramedic. Shorty squinted his eyes trying to see the person speaking to him. He could barely make out the badge. The words sounded distant and smothered by a loud, throbbing buzz.

Everyone around the marina knew how close Shorty had become with the respected old fisherman. His friends saw that he was really rattled. They came over to relieve the officer. One by one, Shorty recognized the familiar faces. The volume of their voices was becoming loud enough for him to hear.

It was a hard landing back into the conscious world. As he became more aware he fell back into denial, shaking his head and repeating, over and over, how wrong, how unfair this was.

Overnight, his life was changed and would never be the same again. It didn't seem possible his wonderful friend, who became the father that he never knew, was gone.

His friends were solemn and patient as they helped him stand. They hadn't seen Shorty when he wasn't in a pleasant mood. Not sure of his reaction, they were afraid to touch him, but walked on either side to make sure he didn't lose his balance. Once he made it onto his boat, he doubled over like his back had given out. With a quiet, raspy voice, he still managed to be polite when he asked to be left alone.

It was so hard for him to look over at Sebastian's boat. He made himself watch as the policemen took pictures and samples of the blood. When they delt with the pistol he noticed they were also looking closely at a lunch bag sitting on the piling. They pulled out the plastic container of leftover food, and took pictures of it. He had a brief moment of clarity and thought it was strange for "Sebastian" to ever leave out any food or trash. He was always concerned about attracting the mange-infested wharf rats to his boat.

Shorty turned away from the painful crime scene and went through his cabin, down to one of his bunks. He laid there for hours, curled up on his side.

It was coming into the heat of the day. Even with the hatch

open and the fan on full blast the air scalded his skin. He didn't notice or care that he was soaked with sweat and that his eyes burned from his own salt. The thickness of the hull was all that separated him from the blood of his truest friend, only a few feet away. More than just a friend, Sebastian was the closest thing to family that Shorty had.

He listened to the activity outside until it gradually quieted down. From his dimly lit corner, he swallowed hard against a dry mouth and took long, broken breaths. When he heard a few of the boat motors fire up, and the popping of a nail gun it seemed like the fishermen were going back to work. It was their way to carry on. Most were silent in consideration to the painful start of the day.

Shorty stepped out on the open deck like someone who was waking from a long sleep. But for those hours he hardly closed his eyes for even a blink. He almost allowed himself the fantasy of seeing Sebastian and the bird, like every day before. But this once happy part of the docks seemed empty and lifeless.

Most of Sebastian's boat was covered with a blue tarp. The yellow crime scene tape remained. The crowd had thinned out, leaving a few law-enforcement people intent on completing their unpleasant job, trying not to show their frustration with this all too familiar scene. A few of his friends returned to check up on him. They sat on his boat and stayed quiet, waiting to hear what the defeated looking captain might say.

For decades the fishing marina had the reputation of being

relatively safe. These young men had seen hard things in their life but nothing this disturbing. They admired the friendly old fishermen and were affected by the senseless loss.

Nobody knew what happened. They did know that a big load of cocaine was busted on the north side of Stock Island. One of the guys said that a cop questioned him about Aubrey and Chuck. They had gone missing and the police were really interested in where they might be.

When he heard Chuck's name Shorty felt another cringe, pumping more acid into his sick stomach. More bad news was on the way. He hoped that his friend was somewhere getting high and not a part of this mess.

None of it made sense. Aubrey had a good business. He was a bit of an asshole but was too wrapped up with his work and his gossipy social life to risk it all, on fast, dirty money from a big drug deal. Perhaps Aubrey's smile was a little too big to be real. Shorty felt foolish for being duped into a friendship with someone who could have something to do with Sebastian's death.

One of the other guys started to speak but hesitated. He went silent, as though he didn't want to elaborate on what he saw. All eyes went to him, insisting on hearing more. He reluctantly said that he was there early and watched the emergency medical units do their work.

He went on to say that Falon was shot twice in the chest and was found face down on Sebastian's boat. He had been discovered still breathing but unconscious. They had taken him to the hospital under a police guard.

None of the young men could manage any pity for Falon. Without saying the words, they all seemed to agree that he must be the killer, that he must have gotten what was coming to him. After a pause he winced as he tried to described how badly the old fisherman was beaten. He quickly acknowledged that the "tough old guy didn't go down without a fight." They found his revolver close to his hand.

The event was still fresh and the law enforcement were tight lipped. The details were anyone's guess and the truth was left to rumor. It appeared like Sebastian must have been caught in the middle of a drug deal gone bad.

When Shorty heard Falon's name he quickly looked up. With a deeper octave than his normal voice, he asked if they knew anything more about the red-haired bastard.

There was nothing else to know.

He tensed up, and his breathing became heavy. Hot gusts of desperation burned inside his chest. His hands were shaking as they flexed in and out of fists. It made sense. Falon was the only one around the docks capable of killing a harmless old man.

An ill wind blew across his boat.

Now Shorty had someone to blame and it raised the hair on the back of his neck.

It was probably best to let his mind go to a different place. The hard knot of sorrow was tied too tight. For self-preservation he had to unravel his pain and replace it with the powerful new energy of anger. His friends had only known Shorty as a peaceful man. It scared them to see the gentle giant look so hostile. One of them offered a drink of rum to calm him down. Shorty gritted his teeth as he thought hard about it, but he gathered his wits long enough to take a pass.

Anger was so unnatural for Shorty, he even scared himself.

THE POWERFUL FORCE OF GRIEF

Shorty spent the night on his boat.

He was too claustrophobic to go home to his small apartment and felt the need to stand guard over his old friend's boat, now a crime scene with no one left to protect. He could only reach a shallow state of sleep. His subconscious mind flashed ugly images that had no sensible connection to each other. He was slow to wake up, worn out from the unremembered battles in his nightmares.

He skipped his usual coffee and climbed up to his fly bridge to sit in the sun and feel the soft breeze. Even the friendly forces of nature were no-match for the dark stormy cloud that swirled around his head. It became difficult to find a place on the boat that remained comfortable for very long. When he paced the deck, he struggled to find happy memories of Sebastian. They were elusive.

Bouts of rage began to wash over him and then recede,

like the hammering waves of a nor'easter breaking on a hard rocky beach.

More than anything, he blamed himself for not trusting the discomfort he felt on that terrible night. He could find no forgiveness for not listening to the instinctive warnings that were so loud and so damn obvious. His regretful choice to roll over and go back to sleep denied him a possible chance to intervene and prevent Sebastian's death.

Being mad at himself was only damaging the damaged. He had to turn this exhausting emotion to where it really belonged. Never before had Shorty imagined such graphic violence. In a strange way it gave him relief to fantasize about the many ways he would butcher the evil Falon.

When he would shift his eyes to Sebastian's boat, the anger would descend into the more dark and dense places of his mind. Leaving him tired and weak. Forgetting where he was and seeing only silhouettes of the living against the daylight.

The powerful force of Grief had gained power over Shorty's soul. Only the passing of time would loosen its grip. Time moves slowly for those in pain.

By mid-day he had gathered himself together enough to walk back to his apartment. He wanted to stand in the shower until the hot water ran out.

As he straddled the stern to jump to the dock, he heard a siren from behind the sandwich shop. It was coming from the abandoned building next to his apartment. He knew right away that it must be another part to this tragedy. The image of Chuck stacking lobster traps passed through his mind giving him a cold chill. He began a hesitant walk to the trouble hunting blue lights.

As he came out of the gate of the marina, he caught a glimpse of someone familiar. Across the road, a thatch of sun-bleached hair was quickly leaving the area. Several times over the last year he saw the endangered homeless child, always in motion and quick to disappear into the alleyways. Shorty would try to flag him down but the frightened kid was elusive, wanting to be noticed, then running away, a ghostly presence that was still haunting Stock Island.

Shorty had been through the abandoned building on one of his walks to work. All of the windows and doors were broken out with shards of glass and garbage covering the cracked concrete floor. He noticed a few burnt spoons and melted candles in one of the dark corners with cinder blocks for seats. It was a private, dirty place for addicts to play.

When he reached the building, he slowed to face another yellow crime scene tape. Solemn and silent, he waited for the police and paramedics to emerge from the cruddy building. He was resigned to the coming of more bad news.

A limp body flopped with the jostling of the gurney as they lifted and rolled it into the ambulance. Shorty saw the pale gray skin and sunken eyes, but not having the face covered was a weak promise of life. He noticed the unique tattoo of a beautiful lady with butter fly wings on the shoulder of his friend, Chuck.

He stood silent, watching as they whisked him away, racing to the hope that only doctors can give. It's always the inevitable overdose that takes the addict. He saw nothing that gave him any confidence his friend would survive this one.

Another gurney crunched its way out of the same building and on to the sidewalk. They didn't hurry for this one.

Shorty stood on his toes, straining to have a better look. Whoever it was had their face covered and it looked like they were zipping up a body bag. He noticed a protruding stomach and caught a glimpse of a fat hand with a ring buried in the folds of a swollen finger.

Shorty softly spoke the name, "Bruce."

Seeing his demise gave Shorty little sorrow. He was not close enough to this guy to have much. It was more like pity, tempered with relief. Bruce had been living only to die. This must have been some sort of mercy for a masochistic soul. Shorty had an overwhelming feeling that Bruce was paying for sins far beyond any human understanding. He didn't know what they were but surely, he must have deserved the ultimate punishment.

He would hold on to every bit of hope for Chuck. In his heart he knew that he couldn't have had anything to do with the murder of his old friend. He was likely another victim of the evil that happened on the night before.

Several times Shorty thought about giving up on this new

life and going back home where everything seemed easier and safer. But whenever he felt overwhelmed and ready to quit, he had a clear vision of Brie and her soft sweet smile. It was a promise that his finest days were yet to be lived.

Law enforcement was still tight-lipped and answering no questions. Shorty was wearing himself out trying to understand what really happened on that painful night. All that he knew was that Aubrey was still out there.

Aubrey was smart and this made him dangerous. His arrogance would make him capable of most anything. As long as he was missing there would be the potential for more trouble on the horizon.

WINDFALL OF LOVE

Shorty found no more comfort in his apartment than he had on his boat so he went back to the marina where he spent the next two days and nights living like his friend once lived. For now, his boat was home. He impatiently waited for any tidbit of news to the ongoing mystery.

Thinking that working on his traps might take his mind in a better direction he stood in the shade and pried off the damaged slats, replacing them with new. Several times, the hammer hit his fingers instead of the nail. When he tried to count the finished ones, he lost count and had to keep starting over. The simple, mundane chores he would normally do with ease were now tricky and frustrating. He couldn't understand what was happening to his old dependable skills.

He still hadn't seen Brie or any of Sebastian's family. He could only wonder how she was handling such a loss, and it worried him. For now, there wasn't anything he could do to help her. This doubled his feeling of helplessness.

During the past few painful days visions of her pretty smile broke through. They didn't stay for long but lifted his spirits enough to take a long deep breath, oxygen for his suffocating depression. He knew he was crazy to be so taken with someone that he hardly knew. It was a risk setting himself up for rejection. That would be all he needed on top of everything else. But she was the only light he could see. Now more than ever he needed to believe that happiness could once again be possible.

His instincts seemed to be telling him that it was okay to have faith in what he was hoping for. This time, and from here on out, he would listen for the occasional whisper in his head. He would trust the mysterious sensations when they interrupted his reasoning. Perhaps someday he would become as intuitive as the wise old fisherman once was.

From across the water, a cool gust of air raised goosebumps on his arms and made him look to the sky. It was Pancho, soaring in a tight circle over the old fisherman's boat. Shorty watched until his neck ached. The bird quit, and reluctantly moved on.

He wondered if the wild bird was missing the food source or if it actually had a feeling for the kindly old fisherman. Maybe he was trying to understand what happened to the pleasant part of his routine.

No different than the tall human.

While he was trying to find some supernatural meaning for the visit from Pancho he heard a boat motor coming closer.

He turned to see that it was a small, but fast sport craft idling his way. Several people were on board. When he saw her long blond hair, a rush of nervous energy ran through his veins.

He pushed the hair back from his face and realized how sweaty and grubby he was from boat living. So, he quickly slipped into his cabin and cleaned up with a cool, wet washcloth. Then put a dab of tooth paste on his finger and rubbed his teeth, rinsed out his mouth, and changed into a clean t-shirt.

As he stepped back out on his deck, he saw that she was looking only at him. When they were closer, he noticed that her eyes were swollen and bloodshot from crying. Somehow, the blue sheen of her eyes still came through. Even with a sad face and a heavy heart, she still tried a smile.

That smile went a long way with Shorty. He felt like it was a special gesture that she saved just for him. It chased away the painful clutter that had filled his mind for days. Now, for the moment, his thinking was clear and it was all about her.

As her uncles tied up alongside, Brie stepped over to the boat that was her grandfather's final home. She paused, and then softly touched the low roof of his cabin. She took a few moments to place her hands on his simple possessions, each little thing attached to a precious memory.

Shorty quietly watched as she made her peace. He was taken with her true grace. Never before had he been this affected by someone else's pain. His breath skipped a few times and a tear ran down his cheek. With the corner of his t-shirt, he quickly wiped it away. He looked around to make sure none of his tough guy friends caught him in a tender moment.

He felt foolish to even care.

Holding two leather bound-books against her chest she turned her attention back to the sober eyes of the young captain. When she stepped onto the blue tarp that covered the blood, she stopped and looked down. A tinge of terror came over her face. She paused and took a deep breath. Then she pushed forward, across the very spot where her grandfather had been killed.

Shorty watched, feeling he had known this lady forever.

Her uncles set about cleaning and organizing the boat. One of them pulled down the yellow crime scene tape. He threw a heavy tow rope up onto the bow. The other turned on a hose and took a brush to the deck. It was tough for them to clean the blood and deal with the artifacts of their father's life.

Brie handed the two books up to Shorty, along with the old rusty bucket with the torn net. He reached over for her hand to help her up, but his boat sat so high on the water it was too big a step. He jumped down to the deck of the old boat and gently lifted her up to sit on his gunwale.

When her feet left the ground the swift, easy maneuver surprised her. Now, with the way she was sitting, and where he was standing, they were close, face to face. She reached with her delicate hand and pushed his hair back to better see his eyes. She unraveled her voice enough to say that he "really looked beat."

The sunburned, frazzled young captain stroked her arm and then her cheek. Then he hesitated when he thought that his rough, calloused hand might scratch her soft skin.

She pulled his fisherman's hand to her chest, and held it there.

While he studied her face for the hard history of her last few days, she pulled him closer. With her arms around his neck, she leaned forward and closed her eyes.

Just then, a loud voice from one of her uncles broke the spell. "Time to go".

Shorty looked to the ground and back up to her eyes and said that her grandfather was the best man he'd ever known and he would miss him every day.

Her voice rattled as she told him how lucky her grandfather was to have a friend like him.

She had to gather herself together to show him a note her grandfather left in one of the books. He made it clear that, when the time came, the two leather bound books, along with the old bucket and net, were to go to his friend Shorty.

Reluctant to leave, she slowly pulled away and slipped down onto the deck of the old boat with her uncles.

Shorty looked at the two books and saw that they were journals. He quickly asked her to wait and told her they were too personal, that they should go with her. Brie reassured him that her grandfather must have had good reason to leave him these particular items.

Knowing how close he was with her grandfather it was

uncomfortable for her to explain that Sebastian had requested the old Cuban custom of a burial at sea. It would be up to her immediate family to tow him far offshore and then scuttle the boat with his carefully prepared remains. Some of the older aunts and uncles were firm about limiting the funeral to only his blood relatives. She sympathetically watched his face, hoping his feelings weren't hurt for being left out.

Shorty mustered a smile for her benefit and said that he was fine with it. He reassured her that he had already made his peace with the loss of his friend. Brie told him that she wouldn't be around for the next three days. With a little shyness in her tone, she asked if he would like to join her for lunch when she returned.

It was a simple invitation, no big deal, but to Shorty it was a whole lot more. Now he was sure this could be more than just two people reaching for comfort during a difficult time. She was just as interested in him as he was with her. The promise of spending more time together was just what he needed to hear. It was a hope worth hanging on to.

He blurted out an excited "yes." Then said it twice more.

His anxious reaction made the serious lines on her forehead disappear and gave her a touch of excitement and a good reason for another smile. They shared a few long seconds, swimming in each other's eyes, searching each other's soul, both wondering the same thing.

Even if it was only for the moment, how could they feel so

good in the midst of such a painful time? These highest of highs and lowest of lows were an emotional roller coaster ride for each of them.

When she boarded her boat with her uncles, Shorty stood silent and vibrating with thrills from this windfall of love.

As he watched them tow Sebastian's boat away, he began to crash into a hollow, and almost homesick feeling. The old wooden boat was the last reminder of his friendship with Sebastian and it left behind an empty hole in the dingy harbor water. He bowed his head with a resigned goodbye.

ZING

Shorty spent the night in his own bed. He was glad that he had chosen a boat that was comfortable enough to live on, but he didn't realize how much he would miss air conditioning.

His walk to work felt different now. He stopped at the sandwich shop and bought a coffee and a few unhealthy snacks. He listened in on a conversation of some of the older fishermen from his fish house. They were still trying to understand the loss of everyone's friend, Sebastian. There were all kinds of rumors, but few facts.

Shorty made it to his boat, determined to get something done. Missing his routine for the last few days made him feel guilty for not being productive. Maybe putting his head in his work would distract him from the empty slip next to his boat.

He picked up the old rusty bucket and dumped the old cast net out on to his deck. He wondered what Sebastian had in mind by leaving it to him.

After lying around, drilling his brain with sorrow and

anger, his body was worn out. He was tired, stiff, and barely had the energy for even the light work of repairing the net. He continued to yawn and forced his hands to stay busy.

When he finished the job, he held the center of the cast net and gathered through the folds to make sure it was done right. While he had it in his hands he decided to walk over to where the old fisherman used to throw, and give it a try.

The first toss opened into an oblong shape and caught nothing. He didn't expect much more than that. He figured it just wasn't in him to become an ace with a cast net, a skill he would have to do without. Then he took a closer look at how he was holding it, made a few adjustments, and gave it one more shot.

His face lit up as he watched it open into a decent circle. As he pulled the net in, and saw the silver flashes of bait fish that he captured. He shook his head, hardly believing he had gotten it right. He wasn't sure if he should keep the small fish or release them back into the harbor but he continued to throw the net just to make sure that it wasn't a lucky cast. He ended up filling the old bucket, along with a bigger new one.

Other than those precious few moments he spent with Brie this was the first happiness he had in days and it gave him a little boost of energy, enough for a fresh new thought to penetrate the fog that settled in and around his brain.

Having easy access to bait fish made him think that he should begin trying to coax Pancho to his boat. With that last thought, Shorty realized what Sebastian had in mind. He inherited the means to continue a friendship with the wild bird. His connection to the natural world.

The pilchards he caught in the cast net were also the perfect bait for catching yellow tail snapper. He had plenty to spare.

This was one type of fishing he always had the most fun with. The brightly colored fish were easy to catch on a hand line and there was no dangerous wire involved. It had been a long time since he had gone fishing just for fun, not having to depend on a paycheck. He had a few days to waste before he could see Brie again. It was hard to hold back his anxiousness. He wished those days were already behind him. Perhaps a little trip on the water would make the time go faster.

Most of his land work for the coming lobster season was finished. The only challenge he had left was to find a decent mate. He had his eyes open but so far, the right person for the job was still out there. Although he had built enough new traps to support another paycheck, he was willing to continue working alone. He still had a few weeks left until he had to decide.

Shorty jumped up on his bow to have a clear view of the inlet and the calm ocean beyond. He thought he heard a soft breezy voice, calling to him. Just thinking about leaving the land behind gave him pleasure.

Normally, on the spur of the moment, he would already be untying the boat, and on his way. But lately he had trouble making up his mind. On one hand he didn't want to be out of reach, in case any real news of the investigation hit the docks. Not being sure if any justice was being served was giving him the prickly feeling of anxiety. But he also thought that if he spent some time alone, surrounded by the wilderness of the ocean, the natural world would help him understand these last few days of life-changing events.

When Shorty untied his boat and started towards the inlet, he had mixed emotions. But he sensed a little relief in the distance. He would be entering into a different world, out of range of the troublesome mystery back on land. A lighter mood did appear as he left the sheltered waters and entered the open sea. He was given back that full awareness of being alive.

He climbed the stainless-steel steps up to the fly bridge, the highest part of the boat. In calm weather it was his favorite steering station. From that height, he could see so much more. The sky was all around him and he could easily look down into the crystal blue water.

The bow cut through the glassy surface as he watched the shallow bottom go through its changes. A great barracuda darted out of his way and continued his hunt around a near-by coral head. Then he watched a leopard sting ray flutter its wings to settle just under the sand. Off to his left, a black cormorant folded his wings back and dove under the surface. After several minutes, the swimming bird popped back up, in a different spot, swallowing a cobalt-colored parrot fish.

Up ahead, he saw a swirling tornado of seabirds develop just inside of the reef. Pelicans, frigates, and gulls of every kind fought each other for a spot to dive on a patch of oil -smoothed water.

He slowed his boat and took it out of gear so he could drift over the wild feeding frenzy, spiraling in chaos both above and beneath him.

Totally immersed in the natural drama he had a moment of appreciation for his magnificent life. Not many people could add such fascinating sights to their life's story. He looked down through the water and into a huge vortex of frantic sea life. In the middle was a massive school of sardines, swimming in a tight circular ball. Dozens of big amberjacks randomly charged through the bank of bait fish. The school flashed as one and turned in perfect unison. Grouper, snapper, and every kind of colorful reef fish known to this region darted in and out of the fray. Even the crabs and shrimp underneath it all were scurrying around, fighting over any scraps that made it to the bottom. A few crawfish came out of hiding, flipping their tails, scooting their way through the competition to find a meal of their own.

Shorty never grew tired of the amazing sights that were exclusive to his life on the ocean. He realized he was lucky and that every beautiful new experience was a gift

After seeing with his own eyes how every living thing depends on eating another living thing to survive, Shorty had a revelation. Staying alive always depends on the death of something else. There is an unavoidable price for the privilege of living. That price is death.

Shorty wasn't very big on religion but he did believe in a higher power. He had pondered too many extraordinary sunrises and sunsets to think that there wasn't a God. Losing his friend, Sebastian, made him wonder about the age-old question. What happens after we die?

People of many faiths believed they were headed to a perfect place of peace with eternal happiness. There was supposed to be a place called hell, reserved for those who deserve the raging fire, forever feeling the pain they chose to put on others.

Those who are satisfied with these promises found an extra measure of comfort when they experienced loss. Shorty wished he had faith like this. How wonderful it would be to believe he would once again see people he loved, like his mom and Sebastian.

But he was science-minded. The words of ancient scripture weren't enough proof to make him a believer. And so far, science had yet to prove the reality of an afterlife.

Then again science had not been able to disprove our continuation in one form or another. He wasn't convinced that death was just blackness without time. There had to be more.

Perhaps if he continued to respect the worth of his instincts, he might someday have an inkling of what lay beyond. Listening for that mysterious voice might help him understand his questions with elusive answers.

Shorty decided to run down the reef for another two hours. It would take him a good distance from home but he wanted to explore the drop off west of the Marquesas islands. He was looking for a slight turn in the reef that Sebastian had told him about. It wasn't easy to find, but it usually provided biting fish. If the weather turned sour it would be a short run to the inshore shallows where he could ride it out.

He found the right place on the first pass. Turning into the tide he dropped the grapple anchor on the rocky coral bottom. When it grabbed, the rope stretched tight as the boat swung around with the moving water. He walked to the stern to see the wash of current that proved it was holding.

It was late in the day, the perfect time for catching snapper. Just before the big orange sun slips under the horizon there would a steady bite of fish they called "Sun-downers."

Shorty chopped some of the fresh bait fish and tossed a few handfuls behind the boat. As the chum drifted in the current behind the stern, he saw the water turn gold with yellow tails. He wrapped some electrician's tape around his forefingers so the monofilament line wouldn't cut into the creases of his knuckles. He let the tide pull the line loosely through his hands, his baited hook drifting with the chum, until it reached the hungry fish.

Zing!

Within seconds the line pulled tight. He pinched the line and turned the fighting fish, forcing it to use its own momentum to swim over the stern, and right into the chill barrel. The ice and seawater slush would almost freeze the snapper, and preserve the bright colors to look best for the market. The bigger yellow tails were called flags.

For several hours he pulled fish in the two-to-four-pound range, considered big for this species. It was a fisherman's dream-come-true. The time passed like an instant. He caught himself laughing out loud from the electric excitement of the hot bite.

For a few hours, Shorty was in his own frenzy.

It was the perfect plate size for these desirable food fish that were so popular in the local restaurants. By the time it was dark, and the fish moved off into the deep, he had over three hundred pounds to sell to the fish house. It wasn't his intention to try for a paycheck but it was working out that way.

Methodically he gutted and rinsed the yellow tails with seawater, carefully packing them on ice. He fileted one to roll in cracker meal and fry up, for his dinner.

Later, as he sat in his cabin to eat, he began looking at Sebastian's journals. It felt strange to be holding the words of his friend. He remembered what Brie had said. He must have had a reason to pass them on to him.

One of the books looked newer than the other. He carefully flipped through the pages and saw that it was written in English. He must have started it after he moved to the United States. At first the words and spelling seemed clumsy, gradually becoming better.

It was obvious that Sebastian had challenged himself to learn by using only the new language. Shorty smiled as he remembered being taught Spanish the same way. What a privilege it was to have known such a smart man.

As he scanned the pages he stopped when Brie's name caught his eye. After reading some of those passages he came to know more about her. Indeed, she had been special to her grandfather.

The more he learned, the more special she became to him.

When he came to the blank pages at the end of the words Shorty felt another pang of sorrow that burned his eyes to tears. How unfair it was, Sebastian didn't get the chance to finish his own book.

He turned his attention to the older volume. The pages looked like they were once wet, and then dried, yellowed from age, a few stuck together. He gently pulled them apart, not wanting to lose any of the important words.

The whole book was written in Spanish. According to the dates Sebastian must have started it when he was a teenager, still living in Cuba. It took some time to interpret the para-graph-long entries so he only focused on the ones that had a star marked next to them.

Apparently, a young Sebastian had been hired by an Amer-ican movie company to run errands around the sets. Soon enough, he was asked to play a few bit parts in some of the old classic black and white movies. Though the reading was slow, Shorty could hear the exuberance in the words. It must have been something for a poor boy from a Cuban fishing village to make it to the big silver screen.

As he read more, Sebastian's amazing story began to unfold.

Through his job, he interacted with some very important people of the day. There had been many times in Havana when he sat at the bar, or went to the clubs, with famous movie stars and musicians from the states. He had several funny stories about hanging out with a famous group of Vegas entertainers who spent a great deal of time working in Cuba.

He also became a close friend, and confidant, of a great American author, one who wrote some of the stories for the films being made in that part of the world. This wasn't the kind of writer who sat behind a desk to dream up a story. He was a great adventurer who traveled the world looking for excitement, and finding the most challenging places to be. This raw experience gave him the ability to write stories with a unique level of realism, gifting the world of literature with many classic books.

For several decades, Sebastian had been one of Hemingway's most trusted cronies as well as his personal chef.

In his youth, Sebastian saw the world and dined with the kings and queens of Europe. He not only fished the world's oceans for monster sized marlin and sharks but had big-game hunted for lions, rhinos, and elephants in Africa. They went into war zones and troubled parts of the world. He was befriended by many international people not because he was close to Hemingway, but because he was man worth knowing on his own accord.

It was hard for Shorty to understand why his humble friend

had never mentioned any of these amazing experiences. They were all worth bragging about. He had, from time to time, suspected that there was more to the simple old fisherman than he ever let on.

It wasn't Sebastian's way to need to impress anyone. He kept his wild and worldly youth in his own quiet confidence, thinking that, someday, someone might read his journals and discover a few good surprises.

Shorty had spent most of the night absorbing one amazing story after the next, leaving him enchanted with who his friend turned out to be.

With each entry he read he began to realize that Sebastian led a long, and very full life. This still didn't justify the timing, and the cruelty of his death. But somehow, it was making acceptance a little easier.

THE MESMERIZED FISHERMAN

The sky in the east began to show the soft colors of morning as Shorty was still reading the priceless old book. He would have to find some sleep during the heat of the day.

He pulled out a cushion and laid it out on the engine box under the canopy. Then he turned the wheel so that the anchored boat would shift direction enough to catch the sea breeze. Only able to reach a shallow state of sleep, his mind wandered in random directions. The happy snippets of what he learned about Sebastian's amazing past floated around the raw reminders of his loss.

By late afternoon, he ascended from his drowsy attempt to rest, reluctant to leave behind the euphoric vision he was having of kissing Brie. He tried to remember how long it had been since he had someone to come home to. Regardless of how things would evolve he allowed himself to have that excitement, that hope.

He prepared to fish for a short while on his last evening

on the water. This time he would attach a heavy lead to take his line to the bottom. He wanted to snag some large grouper to add some variety and weight to his catch.

When the dark overwhelmed the last of the sunset gold, he stood at the stern and looked into the wash. It was going to be one of those rare nights when the ocean decides to fire up her bioluminescence. He sat watching the small green beads of glowing algae as they exploded into swirls, like little galaxies traveling on a black sky. Alone on the water, no land in sight, no noise, no electric lights, no distractions, the magic was just for him, his personal show.

A thick heavy grouper fought well against the strong pull of Shorty's arms. He looked down into the dark but clear blue water, and could see the silver streaks of the fighting fish. He already had a dozen in the chill barrel, including a smaller scamp, everyone's favorite. He wanted to give the choice fillets to Brie as a gift.

Maybe this would be the lunch he was looking forward to.

He stopped fishing for a while so he could sit back and take it all in. As he took long deep breaths of pure air, he felt the grip of grief beginning to loosen. His stress was being replaced by the calming drug of natural beauty. Lost in thought and time, he heard a spouting noise in the darkness, not far beyond the reach of the light. He thought it was a loggerhead turtle that had surfaced nearby for air. He looked into the water and saw it was stacked with a vast school of ballyhoo, swimming hard against the tide under his boat. A wave of the slender bait fish leapt into the air, aiming for the light on the stern of the boat. Several had landed on his deck, flapping as though they were still swimming. More slammed into the stern and fell stunned into the eddy that formed behind the boat. It happened so quickly; Shorty had to duck to avoid being hit by the small, skyrocketing fish.

They were fast swimmers that would launch from the surface and land in a different spot. It was confusing to the predators only seeing them disappear from sight, leaving an empty mouth full of water behind.

Shorty picked up the ones that landed on his deck and tossed them back to the water. Keeping one, Shorty just had to examine every life form he came across. He even had a few books on board to help him identify the different reef creatures that came up in his lobster traps. He cupped his hands around the silver cigar shaped fish still fighting to find the water. It had a long thin bill and resembled a mini version of the giant bill-fish of the deep. Indeed, it was a preferred bait for the sport fishermen to troll for marlin and sailfish.

Then he heard several more spouts beyond the ring of light. When he looked down in the water and saw a big shape quickly looming up from the deep. It startled him enough to stand and back up a few steps. A big porpoise surfaced just beneath where he was sitting. It made a slow pass at the stern, and with a slight roll, it gathered one, and then another of the stunned fish in its mouth. It casually moved on, and a second one followed to do the same thing.

Shorty sat back on the stern to absorb the experience.

Unlike the fish and birds in a wild, chaotic feeding frenzy, fighting for every morsel, even trying to eat each other. The ocean-going mammals didn't seem to be in any hurry, nor had they any need to compete for the stunned ballyhoo. In their own pecking order, they causally circled and took turns feeding right up against the stern of his boat, within reach of the mesmerized fisherman.

One of the smaller dolphins with spots made eye contact with Shorty. He leaned over the gunwale and put his four fingered hand into the glowing water, feeling the smooth skin of this magnificent animal as it swam by. He still respected the fact that they were wild animals, remaining cautious as he allowed himself to become one with this surreal event.

Shorty was the lucky witness to the survival skills of another intelligent species. It became clear that together, they rounded up the school of ballyhoo and systematically drove them into the light of the lonely boat, providing the easy meal. Each one of the dolphins knew their part and understood their place in the pod, no different than a pack of wolves or a tribe of ancient humans. They were a social species that relied on each other to exist. Hunting together in extended family groups assured them the most nutrition while expending the least amount of energy.

During the long and sometimes boring hours of driving the

boat Shorty could rely on a visit from the friendly dolphins. They seemed to enjoy entertaining humans by showing off their acrobatics. Shorty would lean out of his window, clap his hands, and stomp his foot on the deck. In response one or two of them would leap out of the water and spin in the air. Other times they would swim backwards, like they were dancing on their tails. For most of his life he had interacted with these familiar animals, but never as close as on this magnificent night

One by one, each of the dolphins disappeared into the dark ocean. The smaller one with spots was the last one to go. Shorty continued to watch the water, truly humbled by the experience.

A slight tingling sensation breezed across his face and along the sides of his neck. It felt like the comforting hands of someone who loved him. It was close to his skin but not quite touching him. A very soft buzzing sound drifted down around him.

Though he was alone on a remote part of the ocean he felt like he was being watched. But there was no sense of danger or dread that would ignite any fear.

He turned to look to the cabin and bow knowing that nobody could possibly be there. For a few moments, he had the feeling that he wasn't alone.

Shorty didn't believe in ghosts or any kind of spiritual encounters. But he thought he might have just had one.

When the pleasant but mysterious sensation passed, he laughed out loud at his own foolishness. But it wasn't a very convincing laugh. He wasn't quite sure what had just happened. He was caressed by something he couldn't see, and it was real.

He would have to sleep on it. And sleep he did, the deepest, and most revitalizing rest he had in over a week.

He needed it.

OLD FRIENDS

By dawn, Shorty had the anchor on the boat, a coffee in his hand, and a left-over piece of fish to munch on. He ran the boat hooked up, and cut the closest course to Key West.

After all, he had a very important lunch date waiting for him.

He steered his boat inshore and skirted the south side of the islands. It was a good decision. He had begun to see a long heavy squall line developing out on the reef, unusual for early in the day. Fleeting bouts of weather could be seen from a distance, and therefore avoided by the faster boats.

The black and gray cloud boiled as it rolled toward the southwest. All along the edge of the storm swirling funnels bounced from the belly of the cloud to the surface of the water until some of them took hold and became massive water spouts.

The daring nature of the young fisherman made him veer his course a bit offshore. Just enough to get a closer look at the small powerful storm. He wanted to hear the roar of the wind. He counted fifteen of the ocean-born tornadoes and didn't get wet.

When he reached the No Wake zone at the inlet, he throttled down to idle the rest of the way.

The fish house was busy and backed up with boats. It would be a while before a space opened up to unload his catch and hose off his boat with fresh water.

He drifted and watched the fishermen loading up with bait and ice. They were preparing to take advantage of the new moon and catch a few yellow tails like he had done. By this time, most of them needed a paycheck.

Some of the men were anxious to see his catch. As usual, they would try to talk him into sharing his lucrative spot.

This would be the only kind of lie Shorty could ever tell. It's a fishermen thing to only share the location of biting fish with their closest friends. For the rest, he would act convincingly honest, and send them in the opposite direction.

As he waited, the light breeze pushed his boat into the basin. He stared at Sebastian's empty boat slip and looked away when it brought back that sorrow that seemed to always be just beneath his surface. He was trying to avoid the anger that always followed not wanting to spoil his good day.

He saw the small red car, parked behind the fish house and had a flush of excitement. He took a deep breath and exhaled into a smile. He was a little nervous but in a good way, like he always felt before another great adventure.

Brie had an arm full of folders, and was walking to her car to run errands. She did a double take when she saw that Shorty's boat had returned. She quickly tossed her work things onto the seat of her car and made her way around to the seawall where the fish are unloaded and weighed.

The long concrete dock in front of the fish house was a busy place, a social event for the wild men of fishing. They were all vividly engaged with telling lies, and other good stories, about their conquests on land and sea. Curtis and Bigfoot were the only ones actually working. They were shoveling ice and dragging boxes of frozen bait from the large walk-in coolers.

Brie understood the nature of commercial fishermen. She found them funny but was already a little frustrated with the flirtatious comments. No one crossed the line, or said anything derogatory but feeling the hungry eyes from behind made her cringe.

It was her first official day on the job. She had to nip the annoying behavior from the get-go. The perfect deterrent was waiting to unload his fish.

She decided to publicly lay claim to Shorty. Then they would all know she wasn't available. Nobody would challenge him. He was beginning to hold some respect around the docks; besides he was too big to mess with.

She had thought about him quite a lot over the last few days. Her grandfather's letters mentioned him, often. She had been intrigued for months before they met. Feeling like he was grandfather approved, she made up her mind that she would get to know this tall, young captain.

With confidence, and a strong show of authority, she shooed

away two of the boats that were finished with their business on the seawall. They were just taking up space, drinking beer, and yakking. As soon as they were out of the way, she tossed a braided line to Shorty so he could tie off his boat. Her shiny blue eyes captured his. Once again, they were connected and sharing the same goosebumps.

When the beautiful young lady with the long blond hair stepped onto Shorty's boat the boisterous noise of the fish house calmed down to almost a whisper. One by one, they turned their attention to where her interest seemed to be going.

She ignored them as she threw her arms around Shorty's waist. The two rocked back and forth together in more than just a friendly embrace.

Shorty was so taken by this magnificent welcome that the world around him wasn't there. He held her tight, grinning until his jaw hurt. His energy joined with hers and for the longest moment, they couldn't let go. Just when they looked like they would kiss ...

THUNK!

Bigfoot dropped a fifty-pound frozen block of bait on the concrete floor. He began applauding and whistling enthusiastically like he was at a big game and Shorty just scored a touchdown. Some of the others smirked and joined in.

The noise snapped the young couple back to reality. Both of their faces flushed when they realized there was a bit of a crowd watching.

A few of the guys gave Shorty the thumbs up and went back to their work. Several others crossed their arms and shook their heads wishing they were the object of her affection. It made for a fun moment on the docks. From then on, when she walked by, the fishermen parted, and let her pass with their respect. She had made her point.

Brie gave Shorty another gift from her grandfather's boat-- the old familiar espresso coffee pot went to his galley. They began a new tradition of starting the morning with coffee on Shorty's boat.

Every day now, if they weren't busy working, they were together building a friendship, exploring each other's histories, and getting to know each other's minds. The connection they felt from the start was only the beginning of their journey together.

Shorty told her tales of his life. Without qualms, he included some of his biggest screw-ups, things he had to learn the hard way and learned the most from. As he confided in her, he used his corny sense of humor to made light of his mistakes and sometimes clumsy ways. He thought it was important to tell her about his failed first marriage. He easily owned his part in its collapse, admitting to being too possessive and "stuck on stupid."

Brie was captivated with his open-book style of sharing who he was. Most of the men who approached her were intent on impressing her with some sort of polished image. They were rarely honest.

Shorty was different, unafraid to show who he really was,

a perfectly imperfect man. She wondered if she had finally found a man she could trust.

Brie admitted to a few of her own little quirks, sharing some of the twists and turns in her own life. She had had a two-year relationship while she was away at school. He was on the football team and she was a cheerleader. It made sense at the time. She wrapped some yarn around his big class ring so that it would fit and showed it to all of her girlfriends. "Going steady" she called it.

He was a nice guy at first who came from a wealthy family and drove a fine car. But after a while, it was all that she could do to be patient with his immaturity and childish demands. Most of the time she felt like she was just a part of his image around campus.

The night she broke up with him they were at a fraternity party. He was really drunk and when she told him she wanted to leave, he got a little rough. A show of dominance for his friends. He grabbed her arm hard enough to leave finger bruises and yanked her off of her feet.

Shorty was on the edge of his seat, frustrated that he wasn't there to defend her. Brie calmed him with a relaxing smile, and told him the rest of her story.

Like a self-professed wild cat, she pulled away from her football player boyfriend and placed a well-aimed, hard kick to his groin.

Ironically, he was the kicker on the team.

She stood back with her fists ready for more. He went down and rolled on the ground, squealing in a high-pitched voice, sounding like a little girl who'd just gotten spanked.

He'd done a good job of humiliating himself in front of all of his big shot fraternity brothers.

Shorty sat back in his chair and laughed. He was truly impressed with her spunky attitude and fearless ability to defend herself. He reached over and grabbed a frying pan and held it over his crotch, enthusiastically promising to never make her mad.

Shorty was interested in her four years away at school. Admittedly, he had never really been anywhere. He was full of questions.

She went to a small college in New England. It was a beautiful little village with stone and brick homes and buildings. There were big old-growth hardwood trees that cast shade along the peaceful streets and sidewalks. It was a green hilly area with high mountains nearby.

She carefully crafted her words like paint colors so he could see a different world through her eyes. She enjoyed watching his face, especially when she described a hike on the mountain to see an eighty-mile view

From time to time, they spoke about Sebastian, always with reverence. They became a source of comfort for each other's loss. It was still fresh damage and hard to find the good memories through the occasional tears. Perhaps with time.

Today they were new friends, enlightened with the discovery

of each new reason for love. Someday, many years from now, they wished the same wish; to call each other "old friends."

CHUCK

When Shorty came through the door of the hospital room, Chuck's eyes opened wide and he tried the best smile he could manage, considering the battle with death he had barely survived.

The doctors were baffled, wondering how he lived through the poisonous overdose. He was pale and weak. But he would continue to know life.

Shorty realized Chuck had no family or close friends. Being confined to a bed, staring at four pink walls, didn't seem to be much of an incentive to heal. It would only be right to visit with him, maybe boost his spirits a little.

There would be more visits for the recovering addict to look forward to. The next time, Brie joined Shorty and brought her smile, one that could cure anyone's gloom. Bigfoot also joined them. His comedic appearance and good cheer shed a happy light across the dimly lit room. Before the long hospital stay was over, Shorty had quite a few people from the fish house stopping in to show their support. It meant so much to Chuck, seeing that people in his life actually cared. It was fundamentally changing something inside of him.

He made up his mind that when his liver and kidneys, recovered enough for the hospital to release him, he would check himself into a halfway house. Weeks of being clean, were something worth continuing. It would be a stable place to work from and go home to.

He understood that he would never get more than this second chance.

During one of the visits, Shorty took a walk down the hospital hall. He glanced down another corridor of rooms, and saw a police officer, sitting on a chair outside of one of the doors, casually reading a newspaper.

Heat rose up through his shoulders and neck. It had to be Falon. It wasn't a big hospital, and not likely that anyone else would have a police guard. Then he saw a nice-looking lady, and three young children, leaving the same room. They were excited and happy about something. It made him wonder why such a beautiful family would be visiting a scum bag who beat down an old man.

Since that terrible night, a month ago, it had been obvious that Falon was the killer. Because he was in police custody it seemed as though justice was being served. But now, Shorty was confused and beginning to think he could be wrong.

He didn't like to be wrong about anything.

And where was Aubrey? What part did he play in this mess?

There had been a recent newspaper article about Captain

Warner being arrested for corruption. It was vague and didn't seem to connect him with the events on that night. It wouldn't have been unusual for law enforcement to censor their internal problems in the media.

Shorty had an inkling that the man with the big hat and fast boat was involved. The nagging feeling of distrust he had for the marine patrol officer kept entering his mind. At this point, anything was possible. Too many unknowns were out there. It wasn't providing him with any road to closure.

Law enforcement was still evasive when asked about the investigation but promised to inform Sebastian's family if there was anything new.

Shorty didn't have the heart to bring it up with Brie. Etched into his memory was the image of her in pain when she crossed the blue tarp. He wouldn't risk taking her back to that place in time.

For now, Shorty's energy was needed to start another lobster season. He had to force himself to be patient with the slow-moving information about the death of his friend. The first two weeks of lobster season was the most demanding work of the year. All along both coasts of south Florida, the loading and launching of a few hundred thousand lobster traps was underway. It was a messy race, and men were drunk on the passion-filled competition. The aggressive boats came close to colliding as they fought over the best spots in the shallows along the reef, prompting a brick or a heavy lead sinker to be pitched through someone's windshield. There were always a few damaged boats and unexplained casualties before everyone had managed to shoulder their way into workable positions.

Shorty was facing another season of working alone. But he couldn't help but get caught up with the traditional excitement. It was fun to watch the free-for-all as he cruised by and headed to his remote hot spots.

Plenty of potential strikers had stopped by, looking for a chance to work on the fine boat with a determined captain. A few were willing to quit a good producer to fill the job opening.

Now that Shorty was beginning to apply his instincts to his reasoning, he didn't get the right feel from any of them. He hoped Chuck might return to fishing. Since Aubrey seemed to be out of the picture, it would be a "Dream Team" for the two of them to work together. During the visits to the hospital, he never mentioned it. He didn't want to lure Chuck back to a place riddled with drugs. There was temptation around the docks, always calling with a seductive voice to a recovering addict.

He only wished a fresh new start in life for his friend Chuck.

The thought of working alone didn't seem so bad. At this point he had the hang of it. He had learned a great deal about fishing these southern waters. Hiring someone else might turn out to be more trouble than they would be worth.

His hand was healed and did everything it needed to do. He was getting used to working without a little finger and noticed that his incomplete hand had actually become stronger and more versatile than his good one.

Even if he did have to continue on his own, things looked more promising this year. Sooner or later, he would recognize the right person for the job. He would wait until the time when it was meant to be.

Brie finally had a little news to bring to their morning coffee. A sheriff had stopped by and given her mom an update about the investigation.

Sensing Shorty's frustration, she was excited about sharing the new information with him. She looked for understanding on his face, when she explained who Falon really was.

He had been in an induced coma for several weeks. When he finally came-to, his first-hand account revitalized the sluggish investigation. His undercover days were over, but as soon as he was able, he would head up the federal law enforcement in the area.

The sheriff expressed condolences from all of the local law enforcement on the case. They had known the likable old man for years.

Falon continued to blame himself for his unlucky timing on that night.

Shorty noticed that Brie was trembling, having to revisit the story. He put his big arms around her, and when he felt her relax and feel safe, it made him feel like a shield nothing could penetrate. He felt warm and complete, to be living his purpose.

He started to change the subject, but he didn't have to.

She switched into a teary-eyed smile, and pointed at Pancho, who just landed on top of a nearby piling. They both watched for a moment. But the aloof bird kept looking the other way. He wanted to be seen, but was purposely ignoring them. After a few moments, Sebastian's old friend flew back across the harbor.

Brie left Shorty in la-la land with a lingering kiss, and walked to her office.

The young captain began loading his traps. He carried them to the stern, jumping on board to stack them forward. The work was automatic, and required little attention. He let his mind begin to grind the new information.

He was slow to the idea that he could be so wrong about someone. He had to admit that Falon's undercover act was truly convincing. It would feel weird to see this guy as a hero, and not an asshole. The man suffered greatly for his courageous attempt to prevent the killing. He deserved respect.

Shorty wished he had paid more attention to Sebastian's obvious dislike for Aubrey. The intuitive old man was always right about people.

Not only did his one-time buddy beat down an innocent old man but he killed Bruce and tried to kill Chuck. He couldn't understand how so much evil could hide behind the friendly smile of a fellow fisherman.

Shorty felt a sudden urge to be alert, to snap out of his deep thoughts, and be aware of everything around him. Aubrey was still out there, desperate and on the run. He could always slink his way back to the marina.

He looked across the basin at Aubrey's boat. It was still in its slip, and it had taken on water from sitting so long, unattended. The bank of batteries had to be run down, too low to work the bilge pump.

After a thorough search, and the gathering of evidence, law enforcement left it for bait, hoping to coax the murderer out of hiding. Everyone knew it was being watched, but no one knew from where.

Tying a new rope on one of his traps, Shorty was startled by a noise on the stern behind him. He quickly turned to see Chuck carrying a trap to the boat. Shorty relaxed and acted like it was no surprise. Seeing his friend step up to the job was a relief, but he had to ask Chuck if he was sure he was ready to hit it hard.

There was no answer, only a big, confident smile. With clear eyes and a fresh wind behind him, a new and better version of Chuck fell right into the rhythm of the work.

He stopped to apologize for the fifty traps with broken funnels from the last season. He said that he didn't help Aubrey do the damage, but he didn't try to stop him either. He felt bad about it.

Shorty had a bit of wisdom fly through his head, and he had no idea where it came from. He simply said, "Time only travels in one direction, and that direction is forward." "Now," is what time it is. He quickened the pace, with the revived energy of having a new partner.

STRANGE BUT WONDERFUL FEELINGS

Sunday mornings at the marina had a lazy kind of feeling. A few of the boats were out front pulling traps; but for the most part the fishermen were either in church or sleeping off a hangover.

The young couple were enjoying the down time together on Shorty's boat, softly talking, and feeling good about how well things were going. Especially now that Shorty had a good mate. It was only two months into the season and his business was tracking in black ink, and the best fishing was yet to be had. He was well on the way to becoming this year's top producer.

The fish house was closed, but Brie decided to get a head start on a few administrative issues in her office. Later that evening she was planning to have a dress-up date with Shorty, something fancy that they both thought would be different and fun.

Shorty had given Chuck the day off because the halfway

house was having a fund-raising benefit. He was doing really well with the job and, most importantly, his new life. It was easy to see the pride in his attitude. He was also spending a lot of time with Sunshine. She was beginning to look a lot healthier and more alive. Perhaps with each other's support they might be able to climb that mountain together.

With everything quiet, and nothing much to do at the boat, Shorty checked in on Brie and began the walk to his neglected apartment. He had some chores waiting that couldn't be put off any longer.

The homeless crew were crashed out for their mid-morning siesta. He picked up his pace to get beyond them before he was noticed, to avoid the panhandling.

As he went by the sandwich shop, he noticed that it was still closed. It seemed like the whole island had come to a standstill. Wide awake on a sleepy morning, it felt a little strange to put aside his boat work. Then he saw that the old pickup truck sitting in front of his apartment had a flat tire.

He could afford a better ride but he was stubborn about keeping the old fish truck running. He thought it best to putz around with the old hunk-of-junk for a while. A productive way of passing the time until he had to get ready for his dinner date.

Still on Stock Island, Ava made her daily rounds through the parking lots of local businesses, checking the coin returns on pay phones and snack machines, and watching the ground for lost change and other possible treasures. At the end of each day, she would gather together whatever she found, buy a convenience store hot dog and a peach soda. Sometimes, there was enough left over for a bag of sunflower seeds to hide for later.

Ava needed to be near other people but not close enough to interact with anyone. The homeless crew on the corner seemed to be her tribe. Too timid to sit among them, she would find an unclaimed piece of shade nearby, listen in, and pretend to be part of the group.

As she was approaching the gathering of vagrants, the warm gentle breeze that felt so good on her face went still. The air got hot. She stopped just short of the group and closed her eyes. Ava only lived in the here and now. Her painful experiences were not forgotten, but hidden too deep to easily find, a blessing of her condition.

Her delicate confidence was shattered by a flash back of one particular violent night.

She stood still, unsure if she wanted to go near the group.

One of the homeless men, who was slumped forward with his back against the fence, slowly sat up and lifted the rim of his baseball cap. Dressed only in filthy cutoffs and sporting three months of untrimmed hair and beard, Aubrey slipped his dirt-stained feet into his flip flops.

Other than his characteristic swagger, nothing about the killer was recognizable.

Ava didn't need to see his face to feel his danger. When she saw Aubrey lift his cap, and look down the street, her panic welled up, pushing her to run. She was confused about which way to go. She spun around, starting, stopping, starting in several directions until her darting eyes stopped on the nearby entrance of the marina.

With barefoot silence, she ran across the road and through the gate. She slipped between the fence, and the stacks of traps, skipping over and around the piles of broken slats with rusted nails, and barnacles until she found a niche in the debris to hide in.

She sat with her arms around her knees and made herself as small as she possibly could.

When she felt invisible, her trembling hands pulled back a little piece of the vine growing through the fence. She spied on the dangerous man across the street, convinced he was looking for her because of what she saw on that scary night.

She was under a work table, behind a trash barrel that looked familiar. She peeked around the traps toward the dock, and saw the piling that used to have the food for her to steal.

The kindly old fisherman's boat was gone. But the pretty boat, the one that belonged to the nice captain was still there.

She would see Shorty coming and going from the fish house and would watch him walk. If he looked her way she would turn around, and scoot out of the area. She had strange but wonderful feelings about the big man with a gentle smile.

Somehow, she felt safer just being close to his boat.

When she peered back through the fence and saw that the bad man was no longer there, she slipped deeper into the organized mess of Shorty's work area.

Aubrey was standing just inside the gate, his hands in his pockets, trying not to look suspicious while his bloodshot eyes scanned the deserted marina.

Ava froze when his head quickly turned, and glared directly at her. His gaze burned. She stumbled further back, behind the traps.

Aubrey ignored the homeless imp and looked over at the office. His cruel intent was carved in the lines on his face.

Like a rabbit exploding out of the brush, Ava ran across the shell road, and then the dock. She landed on Shorty's boat with her head spinning, and her heart pounding the rhythm of all-out fear.

She stayed low, crawling along the inside of the gunwale. She realized she was trespassing on someone's property, something she knew better than to do and had never done before.

Committed by fear, she looked for the deepest place to hide. She entered the cabin and squeezed into a cabinet under the wheel house, pulling the door closed, sharing the dark place with the control cables and hydraulic hoses that respond to the wheel. She rearranged a few cleaning supplies and aerosol cans so that she made a tight fit, wedged into a space that made her feel impossible to find.

She was afraid that the nice captain might be mad if he found her on his boat, but her instincts helped her feel that this was the best place to evade Aubrey. He was somewhere close by.

Hiding unseen on the nice captain's boat made her feel like she was under the warm blanket of his protection.

FOR SOME
CRAZY REASON

Aubrey had been living in a homeless colony on the other side of Key West, a weird little society, with a strange mix of people. Everyone called it Christmas Tree Island. He blended well with some of the parasitic types who lived there. They were all transient outsiders who would never recognize him as a local fisherman from Stock Island.

During his first few days on the run, he had approached family members for a place to lay low but he was rejected, and threatened off of their property. They wouldn't turn him in. Making "dark money" was respectable in his circle but the killings were too much, even for his people. He was shocked when his favorite uncle, who also dabbled in the drug trade, refused to help. His uncle was nervous about another deal and couldn't afford additional heat to come in his direction.

The police were a better problem for Aubrey to have than the people who owned the drugs. The cartel sent a couple of contract killers down from Miami, professionals intent on silencing him before he was arrested and tempted with a plea-deal.

His only real option was to get the hell out of the country. But the roads were heavily patrolled, and his picture was posted all over south Florida. Without a fake ID, any chance of making it through an airport was too much of a risk.

His plan was a loose one. He needed some serious cash and a fast boat. One with a long-range capacity for fuel. For now, the best place for a fisherman to hide would be on the ocean.

The Cay Sal Bank, an uninhabited group of dry rocky islands between the United States and Cuba, seventy miles across the straits of Florida, was a remote area known to most of the fishermen. Grouper and snapper fishing was virgin, and usually well worth the trip, as long as you weren't caught by the Bahamian authorities, with their old, retired American navy boats. The black smokey exhaust could be seen from a long way off. They were easy, and fun, to outrun.

American law enforcement would have little interest in that part of the world. The killers from the cartel would never expect him to go in that direction.

Aubrey still had a few shady associates he knew could be trusted for a price, a good one.

If he could make it as far as Dog Rock, they would meet him there with barrels of additional fuel, then guide him through the treacherous waters north of Andros Island, and into a secluded part of the Bahamas. He would either scuttle the hot boat, or paint over the name, and file down the serial numbers on the engine block, keeping it for his own needs.

Once he was there, he could lay low for years, hiding in plain sight, waiting for his enemies to lose interest.

Aubrey was good at hiding things. In the murky water under the dock behind where his boat was moored, hanging on a frayed cluster of unused ropes, he had a metal lunch box packed tight with waterproofed stacks of hundred-dollar bills. A small fortune that would go a long way in a country where American dollars have more value.

Aubrey was anything and everything that was wrong about a man, but he wasn't stupid. He knew better than to go anywhere near his boat. Even in the dark of night, he would be seen. Besides, the old wooden lobster boat would be too slow and easily caught in a chase.

There was one last person he would dare to approach for help. Captain Warner was his key to the harbor for several illegal operations. He felt like the cop-gone-bad owed him a favor for sending a lot of tax-free money his way.

Long estranged from his family, Warner lived alone in a two and a half million-dollar home on Big Pine Key. There was a dock, with a boathouse where he kept several pleasure boats, including the Gray Thunder, allowing him to come and go freely for his job. He had a four-car garage filled with collectible sports cars, and a pricey new pickup truck sitting in the driveway.

Warner had a reputation for being tough on crime. The ranger style-hat that he wore added intimidation value to his no-nonsense image as a serious lawman. He was a big believer in himself, quite sure nobody would ever suspect his occasional drift to the wrong side of the law.

It was just too easy to look the other way and be rewarded with a big chunk of change, either a grocery bag filled with stacks of cash or product, which could be quickly turned into an even bigger pay-off.

Until the night of the crime, the crooked cop was confident to the point of arrogance with his abuse of power. In particular he enjoyed making arrests for the same crimes he was engaged in.

On that lucrative night, when he docked the Gray Thunder in his boat house, he had a satisfied smirk on his face until he went to turn off his VHS radio. He accidentally hit the scanner. It stopped on a channel rarely used by the police. When he heard the chatter of local, state, and federal law enforcement making the big seizure he was stunned right out of his overgrown ego.

He looked down at the two kilos of the pure, uncut cocaine that was his payoff. He immediately knew that being left out of the bust meant that they were setting him up.

They were on to him.

He suspected cameras were on his property, and probably some sort of tracking device hidden somewhere on his boat.

His first thought was to get rid of the drugs. Still inside the boat house and believing he was unseen, he cut open both packages and quickly fumbled to break up the soapy rocks so they could melt into the seawater. Then, he put a brick in the plastic wrapping and hurled it as far as he could, to sink it in the canal.

What he didn't know, or ever suspect, was that the Treasury Department had been watching him for a long time. No one could have had so much material wealth on a policeman's salary.

The lust for an affluent lifestyle had clouded his thinking, and made for sloppy spending. Paying huge amounts of cash for boats, cars, and houses was a big, flashing red light to the taxman.

A law enforcement officer should have known better. His arrogance became his doom.

For months, nothing happened. All that Warner could think about was the looming nightmare of being arrested, the death of his carrier, and the loss of everything he owned. At night he cowered in his home, jerking awake at every sound, cringing as he watched the occasional headlights crawling up the wall.

During the day he went to work as he normally would, smiling his way through the debilitating paranoia. His act of being a good cop was clumsy, and easy to see through.

Late in the night he heard a knock on the door, followed by the doorbell. He opened his heavy eyes, and laid there for a moment. He was sure that the dreaded time had come. Day and night he had spent grinding his guts about the inevitable arrest and he still didn't know how he was going to respond.

Shooting it out would be suicide, yet that might be a quicker and less painful way to go. He was well aware of what the begrudging inmates in a federal prison would do to an incarcerated cop. It seemed like a bullet would be better than the blades and shanks of a prison take down.

Warner had a reachable gun in every room of his house. He jumped from his bed, and crept along the wall to the front door. He pulled a loaded mini-14 from the umbrella stand, and used it to move the curtain aside enough to see who was on his front porch.

When he recognized the shadowy profile of Aubrey, he quickly unbolted the door, and pulled him inside the foyer. He took a suspicious look up and down the dark lifeless street. Then he locked the door behind him.

Warner rammed the muzzle of his gun into the wide-eyed fugitive's mouth and pushed him against the wall. He was fierce and aggressive as he roared into Aubrey's face.

"What the fuck? Nobody was supposed to get hurt. And now you have the ass to come here?"

Aubrey spit out a tooth in a spray of blood, and with surprising power, pushed back on the enraged cop. He seared a defiant look of pure evil right into Warner's eyes. With a loud, blatant threat in his tone, he blurted out his demands for cash, along with one of the boats. He made it known that, if he went down, he would take the crooked cop with him. Then, with a scoffing grin, he said, "The Gray Thunder will do just fine."

It was all Warner could do to stop himself from offing the scumbag. But he knew that the splattered bloodstains from gunfire in his home would be impossible to clean. More evidence, more trouble to add to his inevitable arrest.

Although he had the means to help Aubrey, it would be the last thing he would do. He pushed his former partner back out of the door with the promise of chopping him up with the assault rifle if he ever saw him again.

For some crazy reason, the rottenest people have the best luck. Aubrey was slippery, by nature but without even knowing it, he had left Warner's house only an hour and a half before it was surrounded by state law enforcement.

Aubrey was spotted on camera but sensed the hidden eyes almost immediately. He ran to the bridge abutment under A1A, and slithered into the water. He swam to the next island, and crossed over to another, not connected to a road. He hid there for two days and nights, clinging to a tangle of tough roots, and the gnarly branches of the mangrove trees.

It was a frustration for law enforcement that they had missed their chance to apprehend the murderer.

They were able to overwhelm Warner and take him into custody, without any violent force.

Having to arrest a fellow police officer was exasperating. The team who apprehended him were determined to preserve the integrity of the department. Taking a rogue cop off the street made their jobs less dangerous. A few of them were angry with the betrayal.

The ex-Captain Warner had a rough ride to jail.

Aubrey had exhausted every possibility for sneaking out of the country. If he stayed in the homeless colony any longer someone was sure to figure out who he was, and collect the reward. He had no choice but to return to Stock Island, and the marina. If he waited until dark, he could risk going to his boat, and retrieve the sunken lunch box of money.

He already had his mind set on the right boat to steal. Shorty always kept his fuel tanks topped off. Aubrey had greasy skills that came in handy for the work he was accustomed to. He could hot wire a crawfish boat as quick as some could turn the key.

He watched, and waited for days. He didn't expect to see Brie go into her office on a Sunday morning. It reminded him they always kept a substantial amount of money in the safe for cashing the paychecks of impatient fishermen. Those who wanted to hit the strip club before the bank, depositing most, if not all, of their hard-earned money in a place that only left them aroused and broke.

Aubrey quickly realized that the quiet marina, and the safe in the fish house were a gift. Changing his plan was meant to be. A bold day maneuver could give him a better chance, with a bigger head start. If he could avoid going near his boat for the hidden stash of money, he wouldn't trip the cameras that would alert the police.

There would only be one chance to get away and Aubrey knew it would take more luck than what he had left.

A cruel smirk crawled over his face when he realized he could have a convenient hostage, a little insurance if things went wrong.

Twisted thoughts crossed his mind as he remembered Brie's rejections to his obnoxious advances. The prospect of taking such a beauty by force, raised the heat of his desire. He always had a jealousy-based hatred for Shorty, the outsider who managed to survive his onslaught on the fishing grounds. Aubrey was empowered by the idea of making off with both Shorty's lady, and his boat.

He checked his pocket for a 32-caliber revolver, not the best weapon to suit his needs, but small and easy to hide. It was deadly enough at short range and without a second thought he would make good use of it.

He leisurely stood, stretched and yawned to blend into the hazy morning. Then he meandered across the street and slipped through the gate of the marina.

He felt a little exposed as he looked across the water at his slowly sinking boat. He backed up against the gate in the shade, and paused. He scanned the docks between the office and Shorty's boat to make sure that no one was around. Other than a glimpse of the homeless imp, the area seemed to be void of people for the moment. If he waited any longer the marina would begin to get busy with family activity.

He looked at Brie's shiny red car, and his eyes turned wild. He had her cornered.

The office door was locked, but he unleashed the abnormal strength of a madman. He kicked the stout metal door next to the lock, and the raw power loosened the hinges in the jam. One more time, and the heavy door flew open.

In seconds he was looking down at Brie, his arm stretched out, his gun pointed at the bridge of her nose. In a quiet voice he said, "No noise. Open the safe."

Brie had to take her hand away from the phone and answer to the commands of this terrifying man. It was all that she could do to shake off the shock, and keep her wits about her.

After she spilled out the thousand-dollar bundles of bills, she stood with her back to the wall burning Aubrey with her eyes. She knew this would be more than a robbery. Brie would never give up more than the money. If this was her time to die, let the fiery Latina side of her blood make this bastard know that he was in a fight.

Aubrey turned the pistol around in his hand and hammered the side of her head until she was stunned enough to allow him to duck-tape her wrists, knees and mouth.

He could smell his freedom and drooled over his captured prize.

ONLY EVIL
CAN KILL EVIL

Shorty fixed the flat tire and then checked the fluids and belts. The old black motor typically burned or leaked about two quarts of oil a week. He bought it by the case, determined to drive his fish truck until it was "too fucked to fix."

A random gust of wind blew across the parking lot, churning up a little spin of dusty sand. Shorty rubbed his eyes and stepped back from his truck, knocking his head on the latch under the hood.

He rubbed another fresh knot as he watched the dust devil send an empty beer can rolling across the parking lot. The can suddenly stopped along with the wind. He felt a prickly heat rise from his skin, different than breaking a sweat. When the chills went up the back of his neck, he spun around, facing the marina.

He was running before he was fully conscious of it. His big heart pumped hot blood, laced with adrenaline from his head, down through his long legs. They made quick work of the short distance to the marina gate, where he slid into the turn, and rolled back to his feet without losing momentum. He didn't notice the gravel ground deep into his leg, and elbow.

He passed Brie's parked car, ducking to see it was empty. With a few more long strides to the office door, he burst inside and was stopped short by the disheveled mess in the empty room. He took a step back, tripping over the open safe on the floor.

The room wasn't completely ransacked but it had all of the signs of a violent struggle. His insides burned with the absolute certainty that Brie was in the worst kind of trouble.

For a few seconds his brain couldn't tell his body what to do. He stood there, grabbing the hair on both sides of his head, ready to explode from his frustration overload, so scared that his whole body was vibrating.

He took a couple of deep breaths, and forced his way forward. He had to believe she was alive. He would hunt the whole earth to find her.

He flew out of the office, knocking over one of the older Conchs who kept his boat on the other side of the fish house. The shotgun he was holding flew from his hands. Shorty snatched up the gun, and stood over him. He tapped the muzzle on the man's chest, and then set it on his chin.

The frightened fisherman gazed into Shorty's wild bloody eyes and screamed he was there to help. Frantically, he explained that he was down in the bilge of his boat, working on his engine when he heard a loud commotion in the near-by office. He said it happened only a few minutes before.

Shorty exhaled, and shook off some of his confusion. A long terrifying moment passed before he believed he had the wrong man.

He stepped over the fisherman and began to stalk his way back around the docks. With the shotgun aligned with his eyes, he hunted between the moored boats and the waters of the basin, working his way around to his own boat.

He kept blocking any thoughts of finding her body from entering his head.

Then, he heard it, the familiar sound of his boat motor turning over, and rumbling to life.

When he saw the bow of his boat gliding through the basin, he knew it was too late to do anything from this part of the dock. He turned around and ran to the seawall, on the far side of the fish house office.

All the boats had to pass close by before entering the narrows that turn out into the inlet.

As he watched his boat idle closer, he pumped a shell into the chamber, and raised the gun. He aimed square, at a dark, dirty man who was driving, from the steering station on the deck.

He burned hotter when he realized who it was.

Shorty never had to kill a man before, but this man needed to be dead. The fire that was roaring inside of his chest had been snuffed out. Ice was fast forming around his heart. The fore-finger of his bad hand began to put firm pressure on the trigger.

Shorty went out-of-body and was watching himself. He saw a different face, a different kind of smile, one that expressed his pleasure at being the chosen executioner.

He had to become a savage to deal with a savage. Only evil can kill evil.

When Aubrey was out in the open, he appeared nervous. His head flailed from one side to the other, looking to make sure he was still unnoticed in the quiet marina. When he saw Shorty standing on the seawall poised to shoot, he pounded the wheel in anger. Being spotted by anyone was a challenge to his escape.

His confidence was still high because he had a fast boat and a damaged, but beautiful hostage.

He sneered and further taunted Shorty, showing his arrogant pleasure with stealing the fine boat.

With one hand on the wheel, Aubrey reached down under the gunwale behind the winch box. He took a double wrap on Brie's long hair, and yanked her to her feet, bringing her into view. With a tormenting smile, he made a humping gesture while he held her in the direct line of fire.

When Brie saw Shorty she exploded into a desperate struggle, trying to pull away from the powerful grip that Aubrey had on her. He was impossibly strong.

Shorty felt a rush of relief to see that she was alive. As long as she was living, there was hope.

Shorty forced his arms to lower the gun. At short range, the spread of a shotgun blast would have killed them both.

Helplessly, he watched Aubrey force Brie into the cabin where he would drive from the helm. It would provide enough cover to keep his captive, and boat theft difficult for any other curious eyes to see.

For that moment Shorty noticed that his boat was drifting, out of gear, and not making way. It was only a few yards away from the edge of the dock where he stood. This would be his only chance, and there was no time to think. Kicking off his fishing boots, he took a running dive into the harbor, blindly slashing through the water. He gave no credence to the thought that it would be impossible to reach the high gunwales to pull himself onboard.

Aubrey put the boat back in gear and bumped up the throttle to idle into the turn towards the inlet. He scanned the whole harbor to make sure he was still blending into the normalcy of the Sunday morning harbor.

When he had seen, that Shorty was actually trying to swim after him, Aubrey laughed. He couldn't leave without taking another swat at the pathetic outsider. He took it out of gear to let him catch up, looking casual, to anyone who might notice.

Shorty reached the port side corner of the stern. He lunged as far out of the water as he could trying to get his fingers on the edge of the gunwale and pull himself onto the boat.

Aubrey enjoyed watching the struggle. He gave it a few seconds, then cut the wheel and tapped the throttle forward, rolling Shorty along the barnacle covered water line of his own boat. Leaving Shorty damaged and bleeding in the water wasn't quite enough for Aubrey's satisfaction. His lust for blood was once again rising. Looking back, Aubrey threw the transmission into reverse and positioned the boat to drag Shorty down into the propeller.

Brie was on the floor next to where Aubrey stood. As soon as his attention was not on her she saw the opportunity to try and stop this nightmare. She rolled over on her side. With her feet together, and all of her strength, she kicked the side of Aubrey's knees.

She had never stopped resisting, never stopped fighting with the evil bastard who murdered her grandfather.

This time, she managed to do some serious damage.

When he caught his balance and stepped down on his leg, it hyper extended, giving out underneath him. It was then that she owned the wrath of a sick-minded man in excruciating pain.

Enraged with her resistance and now unable to stand on both legs to pilot the boat, once again he pointed the gun towards her fiery eyes. Despite the pain, his quick thinking gave him enough pause to keep her alive for a slower, more pleasurable death.

Brie remained fierce, and defiant to whatever was coming.

The momentary distraction gave Shorty the chance he needed to move out of the way of his own boat. When he saw the stern bearing down on him, he forced enough air into his chest to give him the strength he needed to swim against the strong suction of his propeller.

Soundly defeated, it was all Shorty could do to keep from breathing in water. He was broken, but pounded the water with his forearm and fist, as he watched his boat scoot by and turn into the channel. He believed that he would never see her again. He failed with the only chance he had. The thought crossed his mind to give into the swallowing water.

The helpful fisherman was on the phone line with the police but the docks still seemed void of any awareness of what just happened.

Shorty sat on the concrete seawall, his heavy breathing turning to sobs.

His hand found a chain hanging next to the scales. He pulled himself to his feet, and strained to see beyond the jetty. But his boat was already lost to the distance, and probably half way to the reef.

He dropped his shoulders, and so went the rest of his power.

The long narrow bow, of the Gray Thunder slid alongside of the tire bumpers hanging over the seawall where he stood. The surge from the powerful motors backing down startled him back to awareness.

He watched a heavy-set, dark haired young marshal tying off the fastest boat in the Keys. He looked at the center console, and raised his eyes to the man who stood at the wheel. There was a bit of a stare down contest, between both men. For the longest moment, they were locked in a serious gaze.

Falon lost the contest when his mouth cracked a grin.

It was hard to recognize Falon with a buzz haircut and clean-shaven face. He didn't look so damn red. He seemed natural, comfortable in his law enforcement skin.

The Gray Thunder was passed to the feds, and issued to him.

Shorty shifted his eyes to the ATF patch on the sleeve of his military-style field uniform. Then he saw the rack of long guns next to the wheel.

The city police came from both sides of the fish house and, in seconds, they were standing around him. A strong voice asked him to move away from the water.

Falon stood close with his arms crossed, listening intently to every word Shorty had to say, showing compassion for what the young captain was going through. Shorty was loud with emotion, and frantically pointing out to sea.

Falon bit down and firmed his jaw. He quickly motioned his new partner Enrique to untie the boat. Shorty watched them start to pull away from the sea wall. All that he could see was a last chance to find Brie.

Both marshals buried their necks, reacting as they heard the boat-shaking clunk of Shorty's big feet hit the fiberglass deck. Shorty preempted any ideas of them kicking him off of the official boat. He stretched his arm strait, pointing his finger like a harpoon at Falon. "I'm in on this," he said.

Falon only had a second to consider the rules he was breaking by allowing a private citizen to be on board while attempting to apprehend an armed and dangerous suspect. But there was value in having Shorty's help. He would be the best man to spot his own boat. He knew that Shorty had spent a lot of time learning the trickiest parts of the reef. His navigational skills would be of use.

He looked at his partner, nodding that it was all right. He would take full responsibility for the problematic decision. He told the policemen on the dock that he had it under control. He was firm with Shorty, emphatically saying he had to stay out of the way of them doing their job. He was only there to provide an extra set of eyes.

As the open ocean came into view, the three men were overwhelmed with the heavy boat traffic between the island and the reef. No sooner did Falon lay down the throttle to give the Gray Thunder its speed, than he had to make a wide swerve to miss a jet ski with an oblivious driver.

It was a busy weekend on the ocean. Pleasure craft of all kinds were enjoying the emerald water, and warm blue skies. There was a bill fish tournament adding no less than fifty sport boats to the horizon.

Spotting the craw fish boat in that much traffic would be close to impossible. Shorty hung off to the side of the center console and strained against the wind to see into the blurry distance. Within a few minutes, the urgent search in his eyes landed on an indiscernible speck on the horizon. His heart knew better than his eyes. This was his boat.

He lined up his arm with Pelican Shoals and shouted at the marshal to make his course in that direction.

THE MIGHTY OCEAN

The reef near Key West had a few places that were too dangerous for boaters to cross, where the jagged coral lies inches below or just above the water. The shoals were actually easier to see when the weather was rough, and the deep-water swells crash over the porous living, and dead rocks. These tricky little pieces of the ocean would rip the bottom out of any boat. Most people avoided them, taking the longer way around when crossing over to the blue water.

Experienced lobster men knew how to navigate the treacherous shallows. Setting traps in the white sandy holes, just inside the rocks was dicey but inviting. Early in the season, they held a lot of lobster.

Pelican shoals was directly in line with Aubrey's course to the Cay Sal bank. He was hell-bent to reach the open water where he could disappear beyond the horizon. His lifetime of fishing the shallows made him confident enough to cross the rocks rather than waste any time going around. He calculated that they would be an obstacle, or at least delay, anyone who might be on his tail.

Aubrey had been keeping Brie bound and sitting against the hatch that went down to the bunks. For the moment, she was restrained. But she was gathering strength for her next battle. She never stopped trying to kill him with her angry eyes.

Despite his experience with the shallows, he had to hang out of the side window to see the bottom. It took all of his concentration to find his way through the narrow, crooked channels with boat killing rocks on either side.

With his attention away from her, Brie saw the moment as her last chance to do something. She found a good use for the fake nails she had put on, and polished for her fancy date with Shorty. They were sharp enough to start a small rip in the duck-tape that held her hands behind her back. She was careful to appear still, while her nimble hands struggled to be free from the sticky bindings.

Suddenly, there was a loud pop that came from under the wheel. Aubrey was stunned as he looked down at the dash. He tried the gear lever and it didn't respond to forward or reverse. The boat was powerless against the swells that were breaking over the shoals.

Aubrey's unshakable confidence was slapped down by the hand of the ocean. His arrogance quickly melted into fear, humbled by the greatest force on earth. He was pitiful and childlike as he struggled to find a way out of his own trap. He had a broken control cable and it would take too much time to fix. He went for the cabinet under the helm, hoping to manually engage the gear before the killer shoals would have him.

The second he opened the cabinet, a high-pressure steam of wasp and hornet spray hit him, smack in the middle of his face.

Ava closed her eyes and turned her head away as she held her arm straight and pressed the nozzle of the insecticide until it was empty. She dropped the can and struggled to squeeze deeper into the cabinet between the cables and hydraulic hoses. Shaking, and covering her head, she waited for the pain of punishment to lash at her.

Aubrey's horrific screams vibrated the walls of the cabin.

He fell backwards and tried to catch his balance but his broken knee collapsed once again. He fell to the floor, frantically clawing at his eyes and face. His lungs tightened up as he gasped for air. He was in a blind rage.

Brie ripped the last of the tape from her knees and crawled over to the cabinet. The presence of the child came from out of nowhere. Despite her dangerous situation her mind was quick, and focused.

She softly stroked the cheek of the terrified child, and cooed, "You're safe now."

Ava rolled her welled up eyes to the pretty lady who was always with the nice captain. She instantly found trust.

Brie put her finger to her lips and eased Ava into understanding that she had to stay quiet. She forced her own smile, nodding reassuringly, as she closed the cabinet door.

She evaded the still blinded and struggling killer as she made her way to the wheel.

The boat slammed sideways into the reef, waiting for the next wave to roll through. The harsh crunch was the most dangerous sound a fisherman can hear. It cut through Aubrey's agony, and cleared his burning eyes enough to see shadows.

Brie caught her balance and reached down beside the wheel where she knew Shorty kept his emergency gear. Her hand found a red plastic flare gun with four twelve-gauge shells attached to the handle.

She didn't like guns, and had very little experience with them. She had to overrule the doubts that were flying through her head. This was it, the last chance she would have. It would be a one-shot deal and she wasn't sure if the emergency device was powerful enough to stop a man, especially one crazed with pain. She also thought about the risk of setting Shorty's boat on fire.

She glanced at the cabinet and realized there was more than her own life at risk. A most powerful protective instinct took over, giving her a new level of strength. She had the mysterious young girl to protect.

Aubrey still had a horrible gasping sound to his breathing but now he could see, and his blood red eyes glared at Brie. Through his flooding tears, and pouring nose, he still had the power to pull off a frightening smile.

Brie forced herself to be perfectly calm. She returned his look with a matter-of-fact seriousness, as she cocked the loaded flare gun.

Aubrey quickly fumbled through the loose pockets of his cut-offs for his own gun.

Brie stood in front of the cabinet that hid the child. She aimed at the bastard's chest, not flinching as she pulled the trigger. The wad of burning phosphorus hit him just left of his center. It was a surprisingly powerful round, picking him up, off of his feet, and flinging him backwards through the door, where he spilled out onto the open deck.

The Gray Thunder had closed the distance to Shorty's boat in minutes, those short minutes feeling like hours to a man whose heart, whose whole world, could be dying during any one of those minutes.

The marshals became uneasy as they closed in, seeing Shorty's boat was lying sideways across the rocks. The big swells from the deep water, slammed into its side, pushing it onto the worst part of the shoals.

The doomed boat appeared abandoned but through the scope of his sniper's rifle Enrique saw movement in the cabin.

Falon throttled down, asking Shorty if he knew the way through the rocks. Timing wouldn't allow them to go all the way around, and approach from the deeper side.

Shorty, dragging his eyes from his boat, desperate to know if she was still alive, jumped up to the bow, letting his sea legs bend with the swells. He shaded his eyes to locate the nine-foot stake, the only navigational marker close enough to help get a bearing. He looked down into the shallow water ahead and guided them through the deeper grooves between the rocks. They scrapped bottom, and had to back down several times, but his directions were accurate. They were able to get within thirty feet of Shorty's boat, and still float freely.

Shorty's heart leapt when he saw a flash of Brie's blond hair close to the helm of his fractured boat.

He couldn't take it anymore. Falon had his eyes on the shallow bottom, keeping the Gray Thunder from getting hung up. Enrique was focused on his rifle scope, trained to wait for the perfect shot.

Shorty slipped into the water despite the commands from both marshals to get his "ass back on the boat."

He was able to swim a few feet before the bottom came up and scraped his belly. The pain made him realize he was in a dreaded patch of fire coral. He yelled out as he stood up, and ran barefoot across the poisonous rocks.

His hands hit the gunwale and he hurdled onto his deck at the same instant Aubrey burst backwards through the cabin door, shrieking, and slapping his chest.

The flare exploded and sizzled. The mortally wounded killer fell to the deck, flopping like a freshly caught shark. The rank smell of burning flesh rolled over the boat.

Shorty pounced on the wild killer. He rolled him over, holding him flat to the deck. His four-fingered hand was like an all-powerful claw around Aubrey's throat. He cocked his other fist, loading his entire weight behind it.

Then, he stopped.

Aubrey arched his back and glared one last bit of hatred at Shorty. Then, his evil energy dissipated, leaving behind the smokey eyes of death.

Falon pulled himself up on the boat, soaking wet, with his boots full of water. He grabbed Shorty by the arm, dragging him away from the dead man.

Falon kept his gun on Aubrey, circling several times until he was sure there wouldn't be a final lashing out, a habit learned from experience.

The loud "whomp-whomp" of a coast guard helicopter hovered overhead, its wind ruffling the surface around the shoals. The waves were beginning to slosh across the deck, diluting and washing away the bloody trail from Shorty. The deep cuts on his feet were beginning to sear from the poison.

But he couldn't feel anything. He could only see her. Everything else was a blur. His eyes were still trying to convince his mind.

She was alive.

Brie was sitting in the doorway of the cabin, shivering, and starring at the smoldering dead man. Behind her, the timid face of the homeless child appeared, and then stooped to be near her. Brie came out of her daze and put her arm around Ava, like an invincible mother, defending her child.

Then, she saw Shorty, so terribly beaten, struggling to reach her.

The boat rolled almost to the brink of capsizing, causing him to slide in the wash. He was carried to her.

He wrapped his arms around both Brie and Ava. With his back against the jam, he held them firmly in the doorway of his cabin, keeping them with the boat.

Even the mighty ocean couldn't break his embrace.

PANCHO TOOK THE FISH

Shorty was the first one to make it to the top of the trail. When he reached the big flat rock, and the viewing platform the whole sky opened up, and showed him the distance, like he had never seen before.

He never could have imagined it, but for years he tried. The view from the mountain top was almost too grand, too magnificent for his eyes. For a few seconds he had to stabilize a slight bout of dizziness.

He held back on taking in his first long look at such a sight. He found an empty picnic table, and loosened the straps of the papoose he carried, where he had an even better treat for his eyes.

His big rough hands gently lifted his tiny baby girl. Holding her face against his, together they shared the panorama. He sat, cradling his baby girl between his forearms, on his legs. They were face to face. He was determined to be the first one to see her smile. Or at least be the witness to what could be considered a smile.

Four-month-old babies don't do very much. Most every little expression, or noise, is a first.

Shorty thought he saw a glint of blue in her infant eyes. It made him smile that she would have her mother's engaging beauty. When she turned her head slightly, he caught a glimpse of familiarity. He allowed himself the modest thought that she would have some of his own look.

Indeed, the sweet baby's face was the blending of both mother and father, a new life created with love, a fresh new happiness for their life. He turned to see Brie, just reaching the top of the trail. Then he apologized for leaving her behind. He was just too excited to slow his long legs down.

She stiffened up, and over dramatized her exhaustion, by monster walking. Still a little winded, she scooted in beside him, and leaned her head against his arm. Together, they absorbed the amazing view, as a family.

They turned to see that Bigfoot finally made it to the top. It was a long steep hike, and he was exhausted. While catching his breath, his big round smiley face opened up in amazement with the forever view.

They couldn't see Ava until she peeked from behind his wide body. A huge smile, and cheerful giggles came from the lovely young girl. She had been pushing him from behind, anxious to reach the trail head.

Because she was too young to be left on her own, the authorities had almost tossed her back into the system. But Brie and

Shorty intervened with a force stronger than any laws. One of her uncles had four children of his own and was given custody of the shy, homeless child until she became eighteen.

It took some time for Ava to find trust. But she couldn't resist the embrace of a fun and loving family. The safe, happy place gave her a chance to understand her disability. The damage that life had dealt her was now healing. She survived to blossom into her own perfect beauty

Shorty had been sitting beside her, one day, watching her doodle on a sketch pad. He knew talent when he saw it. He made it a point to praise just about everything she did. She woke up the father inside of him.

Her realistic drawings found their way to the court and were admissible as evidence. There was no mistaking her depictions of Aubrey and Warner passing the drugs between their boats, right down to the boat names on the sterns. This helped convict the corrupt cop. He was found guilty, and finished the rest of his living days contained with some of the very same criminals that he had put away.

Ava became Bigfoot's first real girlfriend.

From their beginnings he understood the way her mind worked. He made her feel safe, and gave her laughter whenever she drifted into her typical confusion. He took her hand, and walked her forward into the world. They were a natural couple.

Shorty relished every minute of that trip to the mountains. The cooler, dryer air opened up his lungs and refreshed his energy. He had finally been north of Miami and saw for himself that the rocks and trees of a different landscape really did exist.

The feel of the mountains followed him home and the recent memories became a great addition to his favorite pastime of daydreaming. He was already planning next year's trip to another new place.

He yawned and stretched as he sat back in his comfortable captains' chair. The morning routine of checking the engine, and trying to coax Pancho onto his boat was behind him.

He was ready to give up on the matter of the cocky bird. But he left the old rusty bucket on the cooler for another try later in the morning.

He flipped the switch for the bilge pump, and watched for water or oil, a little insecure about the massive repairs he had had to do on the fiberglass hull and his keel. Shorty had given up on his beloved boat. At the time, he was too consumed with the miracle of their survival. But the next day someone from the fish house saw his boat drifting inshore and towed it to the fish house. Somehow it made it over the rocks, and was still afloat. He had it up on barrels in dry dock for almost four months. Chuck stayed with him the whole time. Together, they resurrected the boat, and the business.

He looked over towards the fish house and saw Brie with the stroller coming to join him. She stopped to chat with Sunshine and Chuck. They were in love with the baby, occasionally dropping hints of having one of their own.

The quiet, pleasant morning was interrupted by a scrapping noise out on his deck.

He saw that Pancho had landed on his fish box and was trying to drag off the old rusty bucket. He jumped out of his chair. Of course, he banged the top of his head on one of the rafters in the cabin. This time, he saw stars. The boat was definitely harder than his head. He shook it off and couldn't believe what he was seeing

Slowly and quietly, he eased out on the deck. He grabbed the bucket, and had a bit of a tug-of-war with the arrogant bird. Pancho didn't seem to want to let go. But Shorty was firm and took charge.

Then Shorty felt a wave of friendly energy roll over his boat. He held out one of the baits by the tail and with a soft voice, he invited Sebastian's old friend to breakfast.

The great white heron squawked at the idea of being hand fed but his hunger was stronger than his fear. Ignoring his natural inclination to torment the gigantic human; Pancho took the fish.

The end.

A NOTE FROM
THE AUTHOR

In the early 1970s I was one of those kids who hitchhiked
out of the rust belt to explore the country and find a life worth
settling into. When I finally reached the actual end of the
road, the Southernmost point in Key West, Florida, I realized
that my great adventure was only beginning. Without a vehicle,
or a roof, I walked onto the commercial fishing docks hungry
for a job. The locals who dominated the business of harvesting
seafood were openly hostile to outsiders like me. They believed
that anyone who was from north of Marathon Key was a
damn Yankee and had no business in their exclusive world. But
I was hardened enough from living on the road to force my
way past the resistance and volunteered to repair lobster traps
and cut up the dank raw cowhide bait for no pay other than a
meal and enough beer to keep me hydrated for the hard work
under the hot tropical sun. My homeless days didn't last for
long. I didn't like being hungry and sleeping on an old aban-

doned boat. My persistence earned me a place on a crew with a chance for a paycheck. Hell, I had never been on the ocean before, but in a few short years I became a licensed Captain and one of the top producers of spiny lobster in the region.

It was a rich life filled with adventure but from time to time an ill wind of treachery and violence would blow through the maze of waterways and especially the commercial fishing docks. The drug cartels in Columbia used the busy working areas as cover to smuggle in massive loads of weed and cocaine. For the most part the fishermen ignored what they saw and spoke no words about it. But the dark money brings bloodless men who kill easily to keep it.

It wasn't unusual for me to duck under the yellow crime scene tape to get to my boat. All too often a loud, close rip of automatic gun fire would make me bury my neck and look for cover.

Although Pancho Took the Fish is a fictional story, I was there. I lived that life. These characters, from the very best to the absolute worst that humanity has to offer, and these wild, desperate events are based on my real-life experiences. I wrote it so my grandchildren would be able to tell their grandchildren. This is a story worth remembering.

- The Author, *Rusty Jaquays*